WILLING VICTIM

REMASTERED

CARA McKENNA

Second Edition

First published in 2010

Edited by Jaynie Ritchie

Cover design by Cara McKenna

ISBN 978-0-9977834-5-2

READER ADVISORY

This book contains consensual but intense
rape role-playing scenes that some may find upsetting.

CHAPTER ONE

"WHY YOU WANNA LIE TO ME?"

Laurel gritted her teeth, stared down at the book in her hands, the paragraph she'd been trying to read for the past five minutes.

The afternoon had started out idyllic—a perfect July day in Boston, sunny with a cooling breeze, and a prime, shaded bench all to herself off the waterfront's beaten tourist path. A pleasant escape from her un-air-conditioned apartment and the glares of her bar exam-obsessed roommate.

Then the couple had arrived.

They'd been arguing even before they'd taken up residence two benches down from Laurel. Young, probably early twenties, with accents that suggested both had grown up in the area. Every fifth word that left the man's mouth was a nasal "fuckin'". *Ya fuckin' mothah. Ya fuckin' sistah. My fuckin' douchebag boss.* Laurel sneaked a glance. The guy was white but dressed as though he'd prefer to be Puerto Rican like his girlfriend. That stereotype of a look—baggy black jeans, pristine work boots, awful pencil-thin chinstrap beard and an undershirt, which in this case looked as if it deserved the nasty nickname *wife beater*. The girlfriend wore a similar top but her jeans were two sizes too small, the crazy-low-rise style girls constantly fussed with to keep their ass cracks from peeking.

Laurel tried her damnedest to block them out and focus on her book but it was like ignoring a wasp in her ear. The antagonism escalated.

"Don't you *call* me a liar," the girl shouted and stood, shouldering an elaborate gold purse.

The guy hopped theatrically to his feet. "Then don't lie to me."

She tried to argue but he just kept chanting, "Don't lie to me. Don't lie to me. Don't lie to me," over and over, drowning her out. His tone was half threat, half jeer, and he came nearer with each repetition until their faces were frighteningly close.

"You need to back the fuck off," the girl said, holding her ground but looking rattled.

"An' you need to tell me the fuckin' truth."

Laurel's heart pounded. She wanted to find the balls to say something, to do the right thing, but she was afraid of the guy. He had a mean, dog-fight look about him and the fact that he was posturing made him seem even more dangerous.

A walker entered her periphery and Laurel's cheeks burned, embarrassed to be here, acting as though she couldn't see what was going on. The passerby, a middle-aged woman dressed for the office, promptly took out her phone and gave it her full attention as she passed, pace quickening.

The altercation paused until the woman had gone, then escalated.

"Why you foolin' with me?" the guy demanded, shaking his girlfriend by the shoulders.

Laurel's meekness dissolved. "Hey!"

The guy turned to shoot her a glare. "Mind your own fuckin' business."

"Don't touch her like that," Laurel said, hoping she sounded assertive, glad her voice wasn't as shaky as her hands.

The woman crossed her arms and cocked her head. "What d'you know about it, bitch?"

Oh, awesome. Laurel cast them each a disgusted look and pretended to go back to her reading, praying she'd at least embarrassed or annoyed them enough to prompt a relocation.

No such luck.

"I know you fucked him, so just admit to it."

"I didn't fuck nobody."

Laurel's body buzzed, hot and chaotic. She felt powerless and pissed and worthless, probably just how this obnoxious girl felt.

"Fuckin' liar!"

Laurel heard the squeak of a sneaker and whipped her head around as the guy grasped his girlfriend by her fleshy upper arm, his grip looking tight enough to bruise. Laurel grabbed her bag and fished for her phone, ready to announce her intentions to call the cops, but steps interrupted her—heavy, purposeful footfalls on the wooden walkway.

She turned as a huge man passed, striding toward the fighting couple.

The girl said, "Holy shit," but her boyfriend had his back to the other man and didn't see it coming when a big hand closed around his neck, turned him and backed him up against the wall behind them.

The man dwarfed the young thug by a good six inches in height and fifty pounds of muscle. He was built and dressed like a construction worker—jeans, steel-toes, tee shirt, big arms smeared with gray dust. He pinned the guy against the bricks by the throat until the kid's face turned purple, ignoring the slaps and punches thrown at his arms.

"Let him go!" the girlfriend shrieked.

Laurel gaped.

The man gave the boyfriend's neck one last squeeze, a motion that thumped the back of his head against the wall, then released him, stepping away.

The guy doubled over a moment, coughing. His voice returned as a faint squeak. "What the fuck, dude?"

The construction worker took a few sideways steps in the direction he'd been heading, casting the kid and his girlfriend a warning squint. "Both of you, grow the fuck up and buy some pants that fit." With that, he turned and continued down the walkway.

Laurel shoved her book in her purse and went after him. At least fifty percent of the impulse was her desire to get the hell away from the couple.

She jogged to flank the man, having to crane her neck to meet his eyes. Six-three, she bet. "Hey."

"Can I help you?" His tone was tough to place—impatient or just no-nonsense. He had the accent and the look of textbook working-class Boston Irishness, as though he'd come from a long line of coal shovelers or bricklayers or cynics.

"No, I just thought that was awesome." Laurel offered a smile and took him in on a primitive level, registering a turn-on she'd never considered before—brutish, vigilante justice.

"Yeah, nothing more awesome than using violence to fight violence," the man said.

"He had it coming. And it was way more effective than when I tried to make them shut up."

His pace dropped to accommodate her shorter strides. His size gave Laurel a thrill, exacerbated by the leftover adrenaline of the fight. She glanced at his left hand—no ring and no pale strip of skin where a ring might live when he wasn't on the job.

"Are you on your lunch break?" she asked, wondering who this bold woman was who'd taken over her mouth and body.

"Maybe." He glanced down at her again—hazel-blue eyes, wary in that standoffish New England way.

"Well," Laurel said, "can I buy you lunch?"

Eyebrows rose, brown like his short hair and sideburns and fresh stubble. "Why?"

"Why not?" She grinned at him, wondering if she looked warm and friendly or utterly psychotic.

"Fair point." He turned them toward the financial district, up a set of steps and through the tidy alley beside the huge waterfront hotel.

There was something about him... Not charisma.

Energy.

Laurel had hit an emotional wall in the last couple years and being so close to all that aliveness felt good. It felt magnetic, as if maybe she could siphon some of his fuel if she kept her body near enough to his.

They strolled in silence a few blocks to a shabby but popular sandwich joint.

"Meatball sub," the man said, letting Laurel head to the back to order for them. She waited by the pick-up counter, stealing glances at the table her companion had snagged. He stared out the front window at the passing flow of pedestrians, looking sort of calm, sort of blank, big arms crossed over his chest. The clerk called their order and Laurel snapped out of her trance.

The restaurant was designed to feed people and get them back out the door—the tables were tall and there weren't any chairs, the idea being for customers to stand and for families with small children to find a different fucking place to eat.

Laurel carried their sandwiches over, plus two coffees she'd ordered on impulse.

"Thanks," the man said but pushed his cup back across the table. "Don't drink caffeine."

"Oh. Here, mine's decaf." She slid him the other cup and he accepted it with a hesitant face. She'd regret the swap in a half hour when she felt edgy and restless, but she had an odd, ridiculous desire to please this man.

"I'm Laurel, by the way." She offered her hand. He shook it just how she knew he would, quick and firm. "That was awesome, what you did."

"So you said."

She swallowed and unwrapped her turkey sub, picking out the onions she'd asked to have held. "Where are you working?"

"Congress Street. Other side," he added, jerking his chin to mean across the bridge, probably in Fort Point, a hotbed of renovation and new construction. "Where do you work?" he asked.

"I have today off, but I work up the street. Near Faneuil." *In Faneuil*, she corrected to herself, not feeling like telling such a manly spectacle of townie-ness that she pandered to tourists.

"Where're you from?" He asked it through a mouthful of food, and Laurel found it charming. Having a man actively *not* try to hit on her was oddly alluring.

"I grew up near Providence. I've been in and around Boston for…" She did the math. "God, eleven years. You must be from here."

"Oh?"

"Yup." She decided to flirt, even if it was doomed to be one-sided. "Say my name."

"What, Laurel?" *Larrul.*

She smiled.

He smiled back, tight but genuine. "Fine, busted."

"How can you work construction without any caffeine?" she asked, sipping her own watery coffee. "Don't you have to start at like six a.m.?"

"Sometimes. But it makes me punchy."

The image of his hand around the other man's throat flashed across her mind. "I could see that."

He nodded, focused on his sandwich.

"Are you single?" Laurel nearly clapped a palm to her mouth, so shocked she'd asked that.

He raised his face to meet her eyes, chewed and swallowed before he spoke. "You askin' me out?"

You'll never see him again in your life if he turns you down. Just say yes. "I don't know. How old are you?"

"Thirty-two," he said, one eyebrow hitched.

"Yes, I'm asking you out then."

"Sorry, but I'll take a pass."

The reply stung but she shook it off. "Why not?"

"I'm not your type," he said and took another bite.

She smirked. "And how would you know my type?"

"I'm not any woman's type, practically. That's how I know."

"Are you gay? Wow, you had me fool—"

"Not gay. Just not a big hit with the ladies."

She squinted at him, intrigued. Either he was being serious or he subscribed to a complicated, psychological-warfare style of flirting. "Ex-con?"

He shook his head.

"Drug addict?"

He took a deep, demonstrative swallow of the decaf and Laurel figured a man who abstained from coffee was probably pretty clean.

"Asshole?" she guessed.

He nodded, brows rising again, false smile curling his lips.

"I've gone out with plenty of assholes," Laurel said.

"Then I'm sure you've had your fill." He popped the last bite of his sub in his mouth and crumpled its wax paper, tossed it in a can by the door.

"Give me one good reason why not," she said.

"Redheads make me nervous."

Laurel ran a defensive hand over her ponytail. "It's not my natural—"

"Doesn't matter, and I'm just fuckin' with you… You don't like hearin' no, do you?" He smiled, genuine this time, and the gesture etched cracks all over his tough-guy veneer.

She smiled back.

"Fine." He tugged a napkin from the table's dispenser and Laurel dug a pen out of her purse. He scribbled an address in South Boston. "Friday and Saturday nights, eight to one. Tell the guy workin' that Flynn invited you."

Laurel studied his slanted handwriting. "Okay," she said, wondering if all this newfound impulsivity would leave her by the weekend.

"If that doesn't scare you off," he said, "you can try askin' me out again."

"All right—"

"You take care now. Thanks for lunch." He forced another smile and turned away.

"Bye."

She watched his broad back as he pushed the door open then grabbed her purse and hurried out.

She kept a quarter block between them, trailing him back toward the waterfront. The businessmen who usually steamrolled everyone in their paths parted for him like fish dodging a shark.

Caffeine prickled in Laurel's blood and she decided she liked him, officially. She'd like to be seen with a tall, strong, self-proclaimed asshole, out at a bar. Or better yet, to be visited by him while she was working. She'd like all her coworkers to see him and maybe warn her that he was trouble. As she walked she entertained a cheesy fantasy in which she was the only woman who understood him, the dewy-eyed lead in her own wrong-side-of-the-tracks, star-crossed-lovers musical. Which was idiotic given that she wasn't exactly an uptown princess.

She lost him as he crossed the street and she got stuck with a *don't* WALK sign. He strode through the cavernous hotel archway, turning a corner on the other side and disappearing from sight.

Laurel looked down at the napkin again, at her open invitation. She had to work Friday night, but Saturday she was off after four. Eight to one, he'd said, and she bet he was a bartender. Or else a very methodical drinker.

Impatient pedestrians surged around her as the sign blinked WALK and she joined the crush.

Flynn, she thought. She repeated the syllable a few times, guessing it was his last name. There were probably a thousand Flynns in South Boston.

And by early Sunday morning she hoped to have a date with one of them.

CHAPTER TWO

THE NINE BUS RATTLED over the bridge as the sun disappeared beyond the buildings to the west. Laurel leaned against the window watching brick-lined blocks fly past between frequent stops. The robot voice announced Dorchester Street and she made her way to the front, thanked the driver and exited.

Until the moment her feet hit the sidewalk, ushered her out of the dry, cold fridge of the bus and into the sticky July heat, she hadn't been nervous. Now everything changed.

She was a short walk from that man, the one whose face she could only roughly conjure three days after their introduction. Her throat tightened and she knew if her nerves had kicked in before she boarded the bus she'd have never gotten this far.

Too close to pussy out now.

The city smelled tired and beat, as though it'd spent a long day toiling in the summer sun. She walked a couple blocks and found the address Flynn had given her, a bar with absolutely no pretense. It was one of those one-story brick buildings that could've easily been a real estate office or a laundromat or the sort of law firm that advertised with an 800 number. The sign over the door simply said BAR. The picture window showcased beer signs and the backsides of the drinkers who were leaning on the inside sill. Laurel took a deep breath and wrapped her fist around the door handle, not pulling yet.

Darts Night, Tuesdays, Nickel Wings from 6 to—

She didn't get to finish reading the flier before the door swung open at her. She stepped back as two laughing men in Sox caps exited, oblivious that they'd nearly knocked her down. They made a bee-line for the corner and dug packs of cigarettes from their back pockets. Laurel wasted a glare at them and yanked the door wide, greeted by near-deafening music.

The bar was steeped in a nasty fragrance that'd gone unnoticed before the smoking ban drove its camouflage outdoors—restroom base with fry grease overtones. The dark space was filled close to capacity by bodies and loud, barking conversations. Laurel made her way around the venue, squeezing past a dozen sweatshirt-clad men, a few of whom gave her a cursory study. She didn't spot Flynn and bit her lip, feeling as if she'd made a mistake coming here. She threaded her way to the taps, dodging the gesticulations of beer-impassioned baseball enthusiasts.

The bar wasn't even made of real wood. Laurel leaned on the laminate and caught the eye of the bartender. He shouted over the music with the charm of a carnie.

"Help you, Red?"

"I'm looking for Flynn," she shouted back.

He leaned over the counter and pointed into the chaos. "Unmarked door past the men's room. Make sure you close it behind you."

"Thanks."

Unmarked door?

She stopped in the fluorescent-lit peace of the women's room to check her makeup and hair in the smoke-clouded mirror. None of the stall doors had working locks or toilet paper that wasn't trailing on the tile so she decided to skip a pit-stop until later, when she'd likely be drunk enough to lower her standards.

Beyond the restrooms was a short stretch of hallway with the promised plain door at the end. Laurel pushed it open, greeted by a new set of smells. She stepped onto a landing and pulled the door shut, started down a flight of metal steps toward an open threshold. She left the piss and grease behind, slipping into a headier cocktail of perspiration and something else, something medicinal.

The temperature rose even as she descended. The music faded, replaced by braying voices, weird sounds. Her mouth fell open as she turned a corner and entered an alternate reality.

What had been a basement at one point was now a boxing arena, its perimeter lit by dim red bulbs, bright white ones hanging above the ring. Far less crowded than the bar but still bustling with a few dozen people, mostly men. The fighters in the elevated square ring were carrying on a tired, shuffling dance, both looking exhausted, both dripping sweat. Laurel's fist tightened around her purse strap.

She jumped as a bell clanged. A pale, skinny teenager climbed up and over the ropes, grabbed one of the men's wrists and thrust it into the air. The victory was met by jeers, not claps, the crowd clearly not impressed with the display.

Laurel felt displaced beyond belief, the pheromones drifting through the heady atmosphere pricking up her senses and doubling her nerves. She made a wide circle around the ring. Her heart thumped hard then froze.

The first thing she saw was Flynn's throat as he stretched his neck from side to side, tendons flashing, sweat slipping from his jaw to settle in the cradle at one end of his collarbone. He was bare to the waist, powerful muscles lit starkly by the white light, sultry by the red.

He looked both lean and heavy, raw and bruised and tattooed and feral. Muscles ticced and jumped in his arms as he stripped cotton bandaging off his wrists.

Laurel had no clue how to approach him but another girl beat her to it. Flynn looked up from rewrapping his hands as the woman stepped close, holding out a red plastic cup. He accepted it with a couple words and drank, Adam's apple bobbing with his swallows.

The woman was slim, dressed in tight, dark jeans, tall boots, her long black ponytail falling halfway down her back.

Flynn set the cup on the ground beside a towel and crossed his arms over his chest. The woman put her fingertips to his forearms, stroking his skin as she said something and smiled. He nodded and reached out, cupping the back of her head, leaning in to plant a gruff kiss on her mouth. She smiled and licked her lips as they separated, gave him a little wave and walked off.

Laurel's heart beat somewhere between hummingbird and jackhammer. She aimed a final glance at Flynn, hating him and hating her body for wanting his so fiercely. She felt drunk from the atmosphere and her own chemical chaos as she strode to the corner where the woman was filling another red cup from a keg set on a folding table.

Laurel made a quick inventory of her clothes, carefully chosen that afternoon to appeal to the sort of man she'd guessed Flynn was— jeans and ballet flats and a tank top, her rumpled hair strategically styled to look as though she'd rolled out of bed at noon. *Idiot.* This chick made Laurel feel about as badass as a Brownie.

Nevertheless, she stepped forward, throat constricting anew. "Excuse me."

The woman straightened and smiled. "Hi. Beer?"

Laurel blinked. "Um, sure."

She slid a cup off a tall stack beside the keg and filled it, handing it to Laurel.

CARA McKENNA

"Thanks."

"This your first time here?" the woman asked, friendly, as though they were meeting at a mutual friend's baby shower. Her niceness made Laurel hate Flynn even more deeply.

"Do I look that out of place?"

The woman smiled again and nodded. "You do."

"I didn't know exactly what I was getting into when I agreed to come... What is this, exactly?" Laurel asked. "A fight club?"

"Yeah, I guess you'd call it that. It's a gym by day, but it's definitely not in the phone book. Every weekend it's like open mic night for amateur fighters. And some not so amateur." The woman's eyes inventoried the room, hitting Flynn and a few other burly specimens.

"Do the people drinking upstairs know about it?" Laurel asked.

She shook her head. "Only the staff. I think that's why they keep the music so fucking loud, to cover up the sounds of ass-kicking. And I bet the odd drunk wanders down here now and then, looking for the can, and gets a heck of a surprise."

Laurel nodded, swallowed the lump still lodged in her throat. She couldn't keep up the pretense of chit-chat any longer, not with this friendly woman. "Look, I'm sorry, this isn't my business at all, but I thought you deserved to know."

The woman's brows rose over the lip of the cup as she took a sip. "Know what?"

"I met him the other day." Laurel nodded to where Flynn leaned against the cinderblock wall, watching the match. "Flynn? He's the one who invited me. We sort of flirted a little and I asked him out. I'm sorry. I didn't know he had someone. He made it sound like he was single. I thought you should know."

The woman laughed, the skin beside her dark eyes crinkling and placing her age around thirty-five. "You're cute. Don't worry though, Flynn's not my boyfriend. Hell, I'm married." She held up her hand, displaying a ring.

"Oh. Okay."

"It's fine—my husband knows."

Laurel blinked, unsure what to do with any of this. So Flynn wasn't a shady asshole. Though he did apparently sleep with married women. *With the husband's consent.* That was something. Not enough to salvage Laurel's hopes for the evening, but something.

"Flynn and I just sort of…scratch each other's itches." She made a silly face. "Sorry if that's too much information. Anyhow, it's just casual."

Laurel smiled to hide her deepening discomfort. She drank her beer and both women turned to watch the fight.

At length, she found the balls to ask, "What kind of itch?" The warm buzz of the alcohol and the intoxicating, masculine smell of the place made their conversation feel somehow appropriate. Or nearly.

"Sorry, I'm Laurel, by the way."

The woman accepted the hand she put out. "Pam. And Flynn's just willing to go places with me that other guys won't. Sort of rough places. Well, really rough places. Places my husband's not willing to go, himself."

"Oh."

"Flynn's not afraid to be a bad person. In bed."

"I'll bet." Laurel watched him warming up, throwing punches at the air as his eyes followed the fight center stage. His abs and chest tightened with each invisible strike, making Laurel imagine him above her in bed, thrusting.

She didn't hate him anymore, nor her body's craving for his, but knowing he had a lover and a set of sexual proclivities she didn't share weighed the attraction down. He'd warned her, so no harm no foul. She decided if she wasn't destined to score a date tonight, she'd at least make the most of the trip and indulge in a little tourism, explore this strange, violent microcosm she'd stumbled into.

Laurel down the cinderblock rabbit-hole.

"Flynn looks like one of the bigger guys," she said. "Is he good?"

"Yeah, he is. So good he's probably bored."

She and Pam wandered closer to the ring to make room for the queue forming by the keg.

"Why do you think he does it then?" Laurel asked. "Money?"

Pam shrugged. "No money, except maybe a few shady bets in the corners. You'd have to know Flynn to get it. He likes hitting. He likes getting hit too, I think. He's a bit of a thug," she added with a fond smile.

"In and out of bed, it sounds like," Laurel said. Not that it was necessarily a criticism.

Pam shrugged again. "What I told you, about him sexually... Don't jump to condemn him. He's actually really kind."

Laurel frowned, not sure she was looking to get pushed around under the sheets, supposed kindness aside. She let herself process a hunk of disappointment, sad that her ridiculous yen for a fling with the man wasn't going to pan out. So much for her brief foray into adventurousness.

"It doesn't make him a bad person," Pam said, seeming to study Laurel's expression. "He gets off on being rough and domineering and cruel, but it's not who he *is.*" Her eyes moved to the ring. "Just like me wanting to pretend a man is forcing me once in a while doesn't mean I secretly think I deserve to get raped or that I'd ever in a million years *want* to be. It's all about control—having it or giving it up. It's really freeing, when it's your thing." Pam's therapist-office tone made it clear she'd had to explain this to a few skeptics in her time.

Laurel took a couple sips, studying the man who made her body so antsy with curiosity, sad she couldn't get on board with his kinks. Though thank goodness she hadn't found out the hard way. "I'm afraid it's not *my* thing."

Pam licked her lips, mischievous. "You sure? Anybody can see how you look at him. There might be some tiny sliver of your animal self that's just a little bit attracted to that. Our bodies home in on those things. You can't always choose who turns your crank."

"I don't think I'd ever want to pretend I was being…forced. No offense to you, I mean. It just sounds really creepy."

"No, it's fine. My husband feels the same way you do. Though it's not always that intense," Pam added. "Sometimes just being bossed around is enough."

A flare of collective noise filled the air as one of the boxers took a hard hook to the head.

"Think about it," Pam said.

Laurel jolted as the bell rang and fighters fell back, limp and exhausted. The ref called a winner and the crowd cheered and booed its agreement or dissent.

"Flynn's next," Pam said. "Watch him and try to let yourself relax, and think about what it is you find so attractive about him."

Laurel took him in again. She swallowed. "I'm going to grab another beer. Do you want one?"

"Yeah, I'd love that."

Laurel returned with two fresh cups just as Flynn and another man climbed into the ring, donning their gloves and game faces, looking impossibly tall from where Laurel stood. Flynn wore low-slung track pants that showcased the sinful V of his hip muscles and tight expanse of his abdomen. She wanted to tug them down an inch, enough to expose the dark hair she imagined must be hiding just behind the waistband. His eyes were at once calculating and wild, and an image of his face in the throes of excitement flashed like a dirty movie across her mind—a meanness in that stare, a cruel sneer on his lips, a flare of his nostrils, a heaviness in his lids as he gave himself over to the dark things he craved. Her throat went dry as chalk.

Flynn's opponent was a black guy, nearly as tall as him and maybe a dozen pounds bulkier.

"Corners," the young ref said and the men tapped gloves before Flynn stepped to one side, facing away from Laurel. He had a fierce back, two strong muscles pinched together between his shoulder blades, his shoulders rounded swells above cut arms.

The bell clanged.

Not men anymore. Animals. Circling, anticipating, sizing each other up and sniffing for weaknesses. Laurel's focus fogged up as she imagined those strong arms braced on either side of her ribs, tight, that powerful chest and stomach clenching with rough, selfish thrusts.

Pam nudged her with a playful elbow. "Still not curious?"

She kept her eyes on the fight, in awe of the cold look on Flynn's face. "There's something about it, I know. But it still scares me, the stuff you said he's into."

"I'm sure he'd let you watch."

"Watch what?" Laurel asked, glancing sideways.

Pam shrugged. "Us. Me and him. Tonight, after the matches are over. I'm going home with him. You're more than welcome to come and see what it's all about."

Dear God. She studied Pam's face, so blasé considering what she'd just offered. "I don't know. That sounds, like, *intensely* private and...intense."

"You might be surprised how much easier it is to explore things with strangers."

Laurel took a deep drink. "I'd feel like the weird, disapproving prude in the corner."

Pam shrugged. "We could ignore you. And you could leave anytime you needed to. I know it sounds counterintuitive, but it's a safe place to be. He knows what women need. He's sensitive that way. He can tell like *that*—" she snapped her fingers "—when a woman's not into it anymore. He can with me, anyhow. He knows before I do if a line's about to get crossed."

Laurel didn't reply. Her attention was glued to the match, to Flynn. "Jesus," she muttered a minute later. "His body is fucking astounding."

"You want to *really* see that man working, think about what I said."

A chance to watch that body, doing what it was surely designed to do…the temptation clenched Laurel's pussy and stopped her breath.

Up in the ring, the violence escalated. Flynn and the black guy were trading jabs and blocks, seeming evenly matched. Laurel's curiosity landed a hit of its own, knocking her fear to the mat momentarily.

"What's it like?" she asked, keeping her voice low. "Are there handcuffs and ropes and that stuff? Like gags and blindfolds?"

"Sometimes he ties me down," Pam said, "but not always. Sometimes he just holds me with his hands or pins me with his body. I don't like blindfolds usually. I like watching him." She smiled guiltily. "And he's not really into all the accessories and things. Like, his apartment looks like an apartment, not a torture chamber."

"How long have you two been lovers?"

"A few months."

"When you first started…hanging out, I guess. Was it like instantly hot and mind-blowing?" Laurel asked. A scary-loud whack drew her eyes to the match. It looked as if Flynn had just taken a hit to the ear. She glanced back at Pam. "Did you know right away that role-playing that sort of stuff was like, your thing?"

"Yeah. But we didn't go nuts the very first time. When we started, it was mostly just rough sex. Then we moved to him holding me down, then him holding me and me struggling, and then, you know, further. It's like a pool. There's a shallow end. Or you can just sit by the side in a lounge chair and watch."

Laurel turned to the action just as the black guy caught Flynn hard in the jaw, stunned him a moment and crowded him against the ropes, the top one dragging along Flynn's upper back. The ref shouted and the black guy eased off. Flynn made it to standing, a red stripe branded across his shoulders from the friction, making Laurel wince.

The fight broke up between rounds, the men heading to opposite corners where they were handed cups of water. Or possibly beer. Laurel guessed a person would have to be drunk to volunteer for this kind of punishing exhibitionism.

Flynn fought differently the next time the bell clanged. He blocked twice as many strikes as before and landed more of his own—sharp, taunting punches designed to infuriate, not incapacitate. By the end of the three-minute round Flynn had taken only a swing to the neck and a couple ineffective jabs. The round wrapped and Pam jogged over to be the one who handed him his water. Laurel saw her touching his knee as he drank and offering a few encouraging-looking words before she returned to Laurel.

"Still enjoying yourself?"

"It *is* sort of…freakishly manly," Laurel offered, swirling her beer in its cup. "I'll give it that."

The bell rang to start the final round and it went nothing like the first two. Flynn came out on the offensive and didn't let up. His punches were loud, gloves on skin making this sound like what it was—fists pounding meat. The black guy landed a couple decent shots but Flynn didn't seem to register them. He wailed on his opponent until a nasty right hook caught the guy in the jaw and landed him on the mat. He didn't get up fast enough and the bell sounded, ending the fight after only a minute's action.

The teenaged ref climbed up and over the ropes, one sneaker sliding on sweat. He righted himself as the black guy made it to kneeling. Flynn's face was blank as the kid thrust his fist into the air.

He received somber applause, the sound of undeniable respect tempered by a dozen grudges.

He stripped off his gloves and climbed out of the ring, headed to his spot by the wall. A couple men clapped him on the back as he passed but he didn't seem to notice. The black guy clamored over the ropes with some difficulty and a friend helped him to the concrete floor. He walked to the other side of the basement, rattling a body-sized punching bag with a vicious swing, pissed to high heaven.

Laurel looked back at Flynn just as he looked to her. His eyes held hers a long moment, too significant for her to pretend she didn't understand the invitation.

She huffed out her fear and rounded the crowd to approach the victor. A nasty purple bruise ringed his eye and he was peppered with other little cuts and marks Laurel had missed in the dim lighting.

"Hey," she said.

"Hey yourself, sub shop girl. Took me a minute to remember why I recognized you." He stooped to grab a tube of ointment and squeezed a measure across his fingers, releasing a concentrated whiff of that medicinal smell that permeated the gym. Laurel watched his triceps twitch as he rubbed it into the long scrape branding the backs of his shoulders. Her skin flushed as she remembered how those arms had thrilled and frightened her when he'd been fighting.

"That was...something," Laurel concluded.

"Oh good." Flynn stretched his neck. "I always strive to be something."

"You okay?" she asked. "You've got blood on you."

"Mine or his?"

"I'm not sure. Plus this." She touched her fingers to the now greasy scrape along his back. His skin felt scalding hot and he didn't flinch.

"Just rope burn." He capped the tube and tossed it to the ground.

"And a black eye."

"That's from yesterday. See you been talkin' to Pam. She scare you off yet?"

"No, she said only nice things about you. She…she invited me along. For after the fight. To watch."

His face was impassive. "Did she then?"

"Yeah."

"You lookin' for me to second that invite?" he asked, raising an eyebrow.

"Probably. Are you okay with that? If I wanted to?"

He thought for a long moment, unfocused eyes staring past Laurel's face. "Up to her. But forgive me if I search you for hidden cameras if you decide to tag along."

Laurel wasn't sure if the remark was serious or not and chose to ignore it. "I don't know what I'll decide. It sounds really…personal."

"It's up to you girls," he said and wiped his hand on a rag then ran it over his sweat-matted hair. "I'm just a willing body."

"She made it sound like you're more than that," Laurel said, voice low.

"She makes me out like a saint sometimes. Patron-fuckin'-saint of the sadists. You can make up your own mind about it if you come along."

"What time are you guys leaving?"

"I got one more fight coming up. We'll probably head out in an hour, hour and a half."

"Can I get you a beer or something?" Laurel asked. "Or is drinking during a fight a no-no?"

"I don't drink, period," Flynn said, "but you can find me a glass of water if you're itching to be useful."

She nodded and wandered away, found a water cooler and filled a plastic cup for him. She handed it over, wanting to do more…wanting to press a towel to his sweaty skin and clean his cuts and ice his bruises. She felt a strange desire to *care* for him, to apply feminine affection and counteract all the masculine damage. She stared at the black and gray tattoo that spanned his chest—broad, feathered wings bracketing a tall cross, or maybe a sword. Latin words in calligraphic letters hovered above it. *Quis ut Deus.*

Flynn swallowed the last of the water and looked down at her. "What goes on between me and her, it's not pretty. If you can't stand lookin' at a little rope burn, you probably won't enjoy yourself."

"Do you hurt her?"

He made a gesture, something between a shrug and another neck stretch. "Neither me or her would say I do, but it's rough."

"From what she's explained about it… I'm curious, I guess." *And tipsy enough to admit it.*

"Curious is all well and good but I don't know you. And neither does she. If you freak out and go screamin' about it all over town or the fuckin' internet, you could seriously fuck with the lives of two consenting adults. Three if you count her husband. You follow?"

"I'm not a psycho," Laurel said.

"Good. I don't have much of an upstanding reputation to protect, but Pam's a decent girl. I'd be royally pissed if anybody ever messed her around."

Laurel pursed her lips. "Are you threatening me?"

"I never threaten a woman unless she begs me to." His smile came slow and sticky, dripping with put-on sweetness.

"Well, I promise I have no intention of outing anybody. Asking to come along for the ride isn't something I'm all that eager to shout from the rooftops, you know."

"You asking to come along then?" That smile again, more dangerous than his arms or knuckles or threats.

She nodded and swallowed, wondering what the hell she'd just signed up for.

CHAPTER THREE

AT QUARTER TO ONE, Laurel snapped to attention. Four hours of fighting and a steady infusion of beer had numbed her senses, but all that fog dissipated when Flynn took to the ring.

His final fight was much like the earlier one, seemingly well-matched but ending in a near knockout. She watched him pull on a tee shirt and toss a bunch of stuff into a gym bag. Pam was at his side.

Laurel balanced her plastic cup on top of an overflowing trash bin and approached them.

Flynn spotted her first. "Still here then, sub shop girl?"

"Looks like it."

He nodded and Pam smiled, and the three of them headed for a door at the opposite end of the basement from where Laurel had entered. They walked down a couple poorly lit hallways and up a long set of stairs, emerging in an alley behind the bar. After hours in the heady, sultry sauna of the gym, the city's thick summer heat managed to feel refreshing.

They squeezed passed a Dumpster and a couple parked cars in the alley, out of the dark and onto the sidewalk. Flynn led the way down side streets for a few blocks.

They stopped at the entrance to a hulking brick building—one of the city's many repurposed factories, though this one wasn't ritzy like the slick new condos popping up like dandelions all over Boston and Cambridge. Flynn unclipped a noisy ring of keys from his belt and unlocked the foyer door. He strode to the elevator panel to punch the UP button.

Laurel ran a hand over the brick and studied the framed picture hung on one wall—a sepia photo of the building from over a century before, carriages passing by in the foreground. "What did this place used to be?"

"Molasses factory."

She studied Flynn's sour expression, the dark bruise rising along his jaw to match the one ringing his left eye. The ding of the arriving elevator triggered a mental image of him stripped to the waist in the ring.

They stepped into the car and he hit the buttons for the second and fifth floors. The doors eased open at two and he said, "Hold it." Pam leaned an arm in the threshold and Flynn jogged down the hall to the right. Laurel heard him knock three times then he jogged back.

"What was that about?" Laurel asked as the doors slid shut behind him.

"My sister," he said. "She's kind of a basketcase on fight nights. Likes to know when I get home in one piece."

"You guys live in the same building? You must be close."

"Yeah," he said. "You could say that."

The chime sounded again as the elevator opened onto the fifth-floor foyer and Flynn led them down the corridor to the very end. He unlocked his door and they stepped inside. He eased up the dimmer on a set of bulbs that hung from the high ceiling. He and Pam dumped their bags on a loveseat that seemed to be there for that purpose, but Laurel held on to her purse, as though it might save her from drowning. The door clicked softly shut behind her.

She took in the open loft space, with a small kitchen along the far wall. Three towering, arched factory windows offered a view of similar buildings and a sliver of white moon, and exposed pipes and vents crisscrossed the ceiling, making the apartment feel industrial and stark. A couch and an easy chair huddled in one corner around a coffee table. A bicycle, purple with silver Mylar streamers, was propped on its kickstand below one tall window, an open toolbox beside it.

Laurel's confusion about the bike must have shown, as Flynn clapped her hard on the arm as he passed, heading for the kitchen area. "Don't you go lookin' for kinks where there aren't any. I got a six-year-old niece."

"Ah."

Flynn's generous bed was against the back wall, a navy comforter tossed across it in a middling attempt at tidiness. Shelves stood to either side and above the headboard, filled with books and CDs.

"Have a seat." He waved a hand toward the couch. "Bathroom's there," he added, pointing to a door next to the stove. "We're gonna ignore you from here on out, if that works for you."

She nodded.

"You need to leave, you know where the exit is." He turned to where Pam sat on the couch unlacing her tall, shit-kicking boots. "You want me to shower first?" he asked her.

She grinned. "Not a chance."

He went to the front of the apartment and flipped off the lamps so only the dim, sickly glow leaking in illuminated the room. The orange streetlight exacerbated everything industrial and ominous about Flynn's home, made the space feel at once hidden and exposed.

Laurel took a seat on an easy chair, not sinking in but perching on the edge as her eyes adjusted, still clutching her purse for dear life. Pam drank a glass of water at the counter while Flynn sat on the mattress and took his shoes off. Laurel wondered how he had the energy to do *anything* after what she'd witnessed at the gym.

Pam set her glass in the sink. Flynn stood as she approached, looking twice as dangerous now in the shadowy privacy of the space.

Laurel saw his expression shift, eyes narrowing, features hardening. He reached out and clasped Pam's jaw in both hands, thumbs digging into her cheeks. The kiss that followed was less a show of affection than of dominance and ownership. He pressed into her, chest to chest, forcing her backward until she dropped onto the bed. Laurel felt the cushion under her own butt, imagined it was the mattress, that she was the one at the center of Flynn's attention.

"Strip," he said, cold. In her head it was Laurel who peeled her clothes away, skin bared to the humidity and this man's hungry stare. He stepped back a couple paces. "On your knees."

Those words rocked Laurel, yanked her back into her own body. *This is actually happening.* A part of her screamed that this was wrong— chauvinistic and cruel. Another part wanted to see him served, wanted to be the one at the mercy of his selfish demands.

Pam knelt before him and Laurel cupped her own knees, aching for the rude bite of hardwood boards beneath them.

"Get me hard, girl."

"Yes, Sir." It was Pam who reached out to unbuckle his belt, but Laurel could practically feel the cool metal releasing in her hands, feel the excitement as she unzipped Flynn's jeans.

"Take it out," he commanded.

She tugged his pants and shorts down a few inches to expose his cock. She stroked him, the gesture worshipful, just how Laurel felt. She got him stiff, made him long and thick and ready. Her lips parted, anticipating, and Laurel's own mouth watered.

Flynn's voice came, low. "It's been a whole week. You been missing this?"

"Yes, Sir."

"Tell me."

"I've missed your dick."

Flynn's eyes flashed across the room, boring straight into Laurel's. He held them for just a moment then addressed Pam. "You look hungry, girl."

Laurel swallowed, watching Pam's small hand running up and down his heavy-looking cock. She conjured the heat off his skin, the stiffness of him in her fist.

"Suck it," Flynn ordered. He tugged the elastic from her long ponytail and wrapped that hair around his hand, yanking her closer. "Suck it."

"Yes, Sir." Her mouth closed around his head, hand still stroking. Laurel could tell from her hollowed cheeks how hard she was sucking, could feel that aggression building in her own body. Flynn sniffed in a harsh breath and a vein rose along his neck.

"Good. Get it nice and wet."

She drew him out and ran her tongue up and down the length of his shaft, bathing him in her spit.

"That's right…now more."

The fist gripping her hair set the pace, drawing her mouth down his dick in slow, deep swallows. Laurel suppressed a moan to match Pam's, pushed a rough hand through her own hair, wondering how it would feel to be held that way.

More, she thought. Desire and fear hummed in her pulse and her cunt clenched, impatient.

"More," Flynn commanded, and his hips began to pump. In seconds he had her taking all of him, her lips meeting his base with each thrust. Laurel's neck and face flashed hot, her hands damp as she imagined holding Flynn's sides, feeling the flex of muscle and bone beneath his jeans.

"Good girl. I wanna see you choke on that cock."

More, Laurel thought again. She watched him bury every last inch, shut her eyes and clawed her nails against her own thighs, what she'd be doing to him if she were the one on her knees.

Arousal began to overshadow his callous self-control—Laurel heard it as his breaths turned raspy. She opened her eyes, frozen when she found his attention nailed to her.

He looked back down at Pam and tugged the bottom of his shirt up, giving himself a clear view of her mouth. "That's it. Keep that up. Keep that up and I'll fuck you so hard you'll be begging me to stop."

In Laurel's imagination, she was the one giving him this pleasure, the one who's sucked him so good she'd brought that rusty edge to his voice. Even in the dim light she caught his cheeks and neck and ears darkening, saw the faint trembling of his arms and shoulders.

"Good," he said. "Good." He slowed Pam's head, made the thrusts shallow then drew his cock from her mouth. He stroked his crown across her lips a few times and Laurel could swear she tasted him on her own tongue.

"You love that cock, don't you?"

Yes.

"Yes, Sir." Pam lapped at his head, kissed that swollen skin.

"You wanna drink my come later, sweetheart?"

She gave voice to the thirsty noise Laurel ached to, lavishing more wet caresses on his dick.

"Good... You give me what I like and I'll reward you with a mouthful."

Laurel nodded, parched for it herself.

"Turn around," he said. "Hands and knees."

Pam shuffled in place and braced her arms. Laurel felt the grit under her own palms, Flynn's eyes on her back. He shed his shirt and dropped his jeans and shorts and socks, walked to a shelf. Laurel heard a box being opened, a wrapper crinkling. Flynn turned back, rolling the condom down his erection. There was a stern placidity to his face, that same look Laurel had seen him wear just before the bell clanged to start a fight.

He dropped to his knees behind Pam, their bodies in profile to Laurel. Then he glanced to Laurel and all at once it was her before him, dying to be taken, all that heat coming off his body making her woozy.

"Eyes on the floor," he ordered.

For a second Laurel obeyed, forgetting who she was in all this. As she raised her head she saw Flynn gripping his cock in one hand, the other teasing Pam's pussy.

"Nice," he breathed. "You're always ready for me, aren't you?"

"Always."

"Yeah." He angled his cock to her, pushing in. He made a sound of bone-deep satisfaction. Pam made a different noise—a sharp intake of breath followed by a sigh. His hips set a rhythm, slow and steady.

"You been thinking about this all week?" he asked.

Fuck yes.

"Yes."

"Yes, what?" he demanded.

"Yes, Sir."

Laurel saw his fingers dig harder into Pam's ass as he fucked deeper, his thrusts echoing through her body, through Laurel's. She watched his driving cock, knowing just how it must feel, all that hot, thick flesh taking what it wanted in greedy strokes.

"Good girl," he murmured, and Laurel blushed from the praise, needing it to be for her.

He fucked, steady and calm, for several minutes. Then one palm slid from Pam's ass to the small of her back, the gesture dripping with possession. He sped, pumping deep and fast and selfish.

"Lower," he said, a new meanness in his voice.

She obeyed, dropping onto her elbows, hair pooling on the floor like a curtain and hiding her face.

"Lower."

She dropped to one shoulder, then the other, face and neck wrenched to one side. Laurel imagined it, letting her discomfort be Flynn's pleasure. Pam slid her arms to her sides and he took her wrists, crossing them behind her back and pinning them with one big hand. Laurel held her breath, grasped her own wrist, disturbed and turned on and nervous and *hungry*.

"You want this?" he demanded, and fuck if it didn't feel as though that question were meant for Laurel. She bit her tongue, letting Pam speak for the both of them.

"No," she said, almost too faint to make out.

Flynn turned to Laurel, expression cold as he nodded—the exact moment the play shifted from rough to far rougher.

He grunted in time with his hard thrusts, his free hand running up and down Pam's thigh. He brought it down on her ass with a harsh slap and she cried out just as Laurel gasped. Chemicals flooded her bloodstream, the same confusing mix of adrenaline and shameful intoxication as when she watched a rape scene in a movie. In both cases, no one was really being violated, but she registered that same hot guilt she had her entire life, finding the visual powerful and horrifying but undeniably arousing.

"You like that?" Flynn asked, sneering, body hammering Pam's.

Fuck yes.

"No. Stop."

His laugh was sharp and cold and his eyes darted to Laurel, words stopping her heart. "I saw the way you watched me tonight." He looked back to Pam. "You were dying for this cock, weren't you?" He pounded her fast, hips slapping her ass for a handful of violent beats.

"Stop. Please, stop."

"You think I can't feel how wet you are for me?" He slowed, drawing his cock out, easing it back in, controlled and explicit and mocking.

"Don't, please."

"Shut your mouth, bitch. Shut up and get fucked."

"No—" Her protest was cut off by another hard smack of Flynn's palm on her hip.

"Shut your mouth."

Laurel gulped for air, lightheaded and breathless, assaulted by a hundred conflicting emotions. Her awareness flashed in and out of the scene, torn between red-hot curiosity and icy fear. Part of her wanted to run for the door, but she remembered everything Pam had told her during the fights, about how women came to Flynn specifically for this treatment. There was consent, and a core of respect buried inside the cruelty.

She watched Pam's arms jerk uselessly in Flynn's grip.

"Struggle all you want. Only gets me hotter when you fight it." With that, he let her hands go. He pulled out long enough to wrestle her onto her back before grabbing her wrists again, pinning them to the floor as he shoved his thighs between hers. Even in the dim light, even with her black hair strung across her mouth and her face set in a fearful grimace, Pam was unmistakably aroused. Her eyes blazed up at Flynn's as she flailed her legs, kneeing his ribs as he tried to get his cock back inside her. Laurel felt her own arousal return threefold, felt the floor under her spine and Flynn's weight against her pinned hips.

"Hold still, bitch." He flinched as Pam spat at him and Laurel saw his eyes narrow as though they were mere inches above hers. "You'll fucking pay for that."

Pam gasped and jerked and Laurel imagined his intrusion between her own legs, mean and merciless.

"Yeah, that's what you get." He found a rhythm, graceless now, working against her thrashing body. "Harder you struggle, the harder I fuck you," he warned. "Open your mouth."

She bucked and spat again.

"Don't fuck with me," Flynn said. He yanked at her wrist, making her back arch, making Laurel's ache alongside it. "Do what I say or I'm gonna get mean."

She twisted under his hold and he yanked again and this time her body quieted.

"Better," he said. "Now open that mouth."

Both women parted their lips as Flynn lowered to kiss Pam, violent, hips still pounding. For a moment Laurel could feel his firm, wet tongue taking her mouth, then he jerked away with a gruff noise, released her wrist to touch his fingers to his lip.

"Fucking bitch."

Laurel watched Pam slap uselessly at his slick chest and stomach as he wiped the blood from his bitten lip. Flynn squinted down at his victim, hips going still, his face full of hatred so cold it made Laurel shiver from ten feet away.

Without warning, he jammed his blood-streaked fingers into Pam's mouth before moving them to her throat, pushing her head against the floor. Her assaulting hand froze between them.

Laurel froze too, body so tight with arousal and adrenaline she felt faint. She tasted copper in her mouth and her throat closed up.

Flynn's next words came slow and dark and dangerous. "Now you're going to do what I say. You understand?"

Pam made a noise, strained but coherent enough to tell Laurel she could breathe just fine, that Flynn wasn't actually choking her.

"Right. Now you be a good girl and reach that hand down and touch yourself." When she didn't respond he seemed to tighten his hold on her neck. *"Now."*

She obeyed, snaking her hand between their bodies to finger her clit. Laurel ached to do the same, her pussy begging for it. She held back, reminded herself of her role and made her obedience into an unspoken order from Flynn.

"Good." He moved his choking hand to the floor by Pam's shoulder. "Now you make yourself come, bitch. And I'll know if you're faking. You make that cunt clench around my cock or I swear to God you'll regret it."

Words gave way to moans and grunts as both bodies turned frantic. Laurel smelled the heady mix of sweat and sex and latex, felt the heat peeling off them against her own dampening skin. Her eyes drank in every shape of Flynn's powerful body as it twitched and tightened, his thrusts looking punishing, the brutality real. Her cunt was screaming to experience him, throbbing deep and hot with impatience.

Pam came apart. Her breathy grunts matched Flynn's harsh ones and her legs came up, knees hugging his waist, inviting him deeper. He let her pinned hand go and she moved it to her chest to palm her breasts and tweak her nipples. Laurel's fingers twitched, dying to do the same.

They fucked like nothing she'd ever seen in porn—technically missionary, seemingly vanilla, but the intensity between them was incredible, palpable, crackling with electricity.

All at once that energy was rerouted, shot straight across the room between Flynn's eyes and Laurel's and she *felt* him, all the aggression and strength of his body pummeling hers.

Pam groaned beneath him, head turning to the side as the hand stroking her breasts grew frantic.

"Good girl. Come all over that hard cock." He froze, pushed deep inside.

Pam cried out, raked his back as she climaxed. Laurel's mind swam for a second, lost in the details of Flynn—his sweat-damp hair, muscles gleaming in the city's ambient glow. She breathed in his smell, feasted on his body. She wanted him more violently than anything she could recall, as though the need in her were blinding pain and the only thing that could take it away was Flynn.

"That's right," he whispered, hips giving a few gentle pumps as Pam calmed. "That's right. Good girl." He leaned in, kissed her forehead. The gesture sent an odd ripple through Laurel, seeming twice as graphic and raw as any other intimate contact she'd witnessed in the last ten minutes.

Flynn pulled out and got to his feet as Pam made it unsteadily to her knees. She reached out to unroll the condom from his cock, set it aside and stroked his flesh. Laurel imagined him in her palm. His balls looked tight and high, telling her how close he must be. He took over after a minute, jerking fast and rough, and Laurel felt each bump of his head against Pam's lips. She felt his skin under her nails as Pam dug her fingers into his thighs, saw his need as her eyes stared up at his face.

"Here I come, sweetheart. Open up wide for me."

Laurel ached to see him come but Pam's mouth closed over his head, keeping the moment private, forcing her out of all this borrowed intimacy. She had to be satisfied watching his clenching ass and his tight fist as his hand slowed, had to settle for his rumbling moan as he released. She saw Pam swallow what he gave her, felt her heart stop when his gaze jumped to her face for the briefest moment.

"C'mon." He put a hand out and helped Pam to standing. "Go get cleaned up."

Pam disappeared into the bathroom, closing the door to block out the light and the whir of the fan. A moment later the shower hissed on.

Laurel's stomach dropped and she wondered if she was supposed to go now. She bit her lip, watching Flynn tug on his jeans and buckle his belt. He turned to her, still barefoot and stripped to the waist and looking just as dangerous as he did in the ring.

"Still here, huh?"

She tried to keep her eyes on his face, off his gleaming stomach, tried to keep her awareness on the words and off her pleading cunt. "Looks like it."

He nodded and pulled on his shirt as the water shut off. He flipped the lights on and gathered Pam's clothes, knocked on the bathroom door. A hand emerged to accept them with a thank-you.

Laurel got up, stepping to the windows to peer at the empty street five stories down.

"You dawdling?" Flynn asked. When she turned to try to come up with a pithy answer she found him smiling at her, thumbs tucked into his pockets.

"It's okay," he said. "You probably got some questions. Run away if you want though."

She opened her mouth to speak just as Pam opened the bathroom door, flipping off the light and fan to emerge fully dressed. She looked different with her hair wet, bangs off her face, eyeliner and dark lipstick gone—vulnerable and heartbreakingly human. She turned to Laurel, her voice softer than it had been all evening.

"Did you like it?"

Laurel pursed her lips a moment and nodded. "Yeah. Thanks for inviting me." She turned to Flynn and held his eyes to tell him the thanks were meant for both of them.

"Walk you to your car?" he asked Pam.

"No, I'm just across the way."

"I'll watch from the window," he said. "Go on, it's late."

Oh, right. She's got a husband at home. Weird.

Pam turned to Laurel. "You need a ride anywhere?"

"No, I live close," she lied. "Thanks though."

"Sure. Nice meeting you, Laurel." She headed for the exit, Flynn right behind her.

"Take care," he said, and closed the door. He braced a hand on the wood and leaned into it as if he were thinking, then walked to the windows. He stared down into the street for a minute, raised a hand in a small wave as a car started up outside.

He turned to approach Laurel, crossing his arms over his chest. "So."

"You're bleeding," she said, eyes on the fresh blood shining along the gash on his lip.

He wiped his mouth, smearing red. "You traumatized now or anything?"

She ignored his patronizing tone. "Do you have peroxide?"

He blinked at her a couple times then headed to the bathroom. She loitered at the open door while he crouched at the cupboard below the sink. He stood, a bottle of rubbing alcohol in hand, and Laurel edged past him to root through his medicine cabinet, finding antiseptic ointment and bandages. No cotton balls, but she popped the toilet paper roll off its spool and headed back into the main room. She heard Flynn behind her as she walked to his bed and sat on its edge. He looked down at her, semi-silhouetted. She patted the mattress and he surprised her by sitting.

Laurel angled his head and inspected the cut. He didn't flinch as she brushed her fingertips over it.

"You a nurse or something?"

"No, I'm a waitress."

"Aren't you too old to be a waitress?" he asked, the tease stinging. She hoped the alcohol just might return the favor.

"I'm only twenty-nine."

"Yeah, but you can wait tables in Providence. Nobody moves to Boston to become a waitress. Where'd you drop out from?"

"Nowhere. I graduated from Wentworth." *He remembered where I'm from. That's something, right?* She wet a wad of toilet paper and pressed it to his lip. He didn't bat an eye. "I didn't like my field all that much once I got into it."

"Waste of thousands of dollars."

She frowned. "I had a scholarship, not that it's your business. Is there a humongous chip on your shoulder I should be disinfecting?"

"Sorry," he said, not sounding it.

"What do you care, anyway?"

"I like to know who I'm playing with, and you seem like you might be sticking around." He watched her smear her fingers with ointment before dabbing at his cut.

"Well, I'm a failed engineer who waits tables at a tourist trap in Quincy Market," she said, not meeting his eyes.

"And you don't live around here, do you?"

"No. I live in the North End."

"Roommates?"

She nodded. "I'm pushing thirty and my career's in the shitter and I wait tables and have two roommates. And my longest relationship lasted less than your current fuckbuddy arrangement. Happy?"

Flynn laughed genuinely for the first time and it changed him. It deepened the lines beside his eyes and mouth, revealed his imperfect but white teeth. It also reopened the cut and she glared at him.

"What else have you got?" Laurel touched her fingers to a nasty bruise just above his collar. He peeled up his tee and she grimaced at the array of black and blues—way more now that she was close up. An ugly scrape traced his collarbone but nothing else appeared to be bleeding. Laurel swabbed the scrape and smeared it with Bactine, smoothed a bandage in place.

"Why do you do that?" she asked. "The fights?"

"Same reason I do the other shit you saw tonight."

"Which is?" She crumpled the bandage wrapper in her fist and held his stare.

"Dunno. Just need to."

"Does it make you feel alive or something?"

"Why'd *you* come here tonight?"

She nodded. "Touché."

"You done fussing over me?"

She screwed the cap back on the ointment and nodded again.

"You drive here?"

She shook her head. "Bus."

"Buses ain't running this late. You want a ride?"

"I can call a cab."

"Or I can give you a ride. Come on." He stood and tugged his shirt back on and she followed, setting the first-aid supplies on his counter. She grabbed her purse from the table as Flynn pulled on his shoes and clipped his keys to his belt.

"Flynn isn't your first name, is it?" Laurel asked.

"No. It's Michael."

"Oh." She'd been expecting a little more evasion or possibly a stranger name than Michael. "Well, my last name's White."

"Right. Laurel White, I'm Michael Flynn." He shook her hand curtly. "You've watched me fuck and we know each other's full names. That enough for your first night?"

She offered a snide little smile. "Sure." They left the apartment and he locked up behind them. They shared a silent elevator ride and walked half a block to a rust-pocked white station wagon. Flynn unlocked the driver's side, slid in and leaned over to pull the lock for Laurel's door. She sat down and glanced at him, then around the car.

He started the engine, grinning. "What'd you expect?"

"Not a station wagon."

"I'm the only non-drinker in a bar full of fighters. Some nights I wish I had a minivan for haulin' people's drunk, limping asses home." He pulled them onto the silent street and Laurel rolled down her window, breathing in that ripened summer city smell.

Flynn flipped on a classic rock station and lowered the volume.

"Thank you," she said. "For letting me tag along."

He shrugged and they didn't speak for a couple minutes as he took them over a bridge and through the Seaport District. *Dirty Water* came on, as though they'd just driven into a parody of themselves.

"Think you're interested in what I do?" Flynn asked, turning to her. "If you are, all you have to do is tell me what night."

"Are you interested in inviting me?" she asked.

"Pretty sure I just did."

She shifted in her seat and clutched her purse tighter. "I'm interested. I'm not sure how I'll feel tomorrow though."

"Just pick a night. You can always stand me up."

"You must work early. So weeknights would be—"

"Quit stalling. Just pick a day."

"Okay. Wednesday. I'm off work at four."

He nodded. "Fine. Come over around eight. Or don't. But I'll make sure and be home then."

She nodded and exhaled, feeling all at once relieved. "Is there a...shallow end? You know, to the rough stuff."

He grinned at her. "You need training wheels?"

"Well—"

"Just fuckin' with you. Of course there's a shallow end. You've seen how I like to screw. But it's a preference, not a fetish. I don't *have* to be a prick to get hard." He turned the car onto Atlantic Avenue, downtown looking as empty as Laurel had ever seen it.

"Regular sex is like jerking off to me," he went on. "It feels good, it gets the job done. But I'd rather be doing somethin' else, you know?"

"Are you part of the BDSM scene or whatever?"

He made an exasperated noise. "I can't stand that shit. They make everything so fucking complicated. You might as well be one of those Civil-fucking-War…" He twirled his hand, searching for the word.

"Reenactors?"

He snapped his fingers at her. "Three points. Anyhow, I just like stuff a lot of women don't, so I have to make sure I find the ones who do. Like, really do. Do you have a man someplace?"

"No."

"Good," he said.

"Pam does."

"I know, and I won't lie, it bugs me."

"She said he knows about you guys."

"Yeah, and I believe her. But it'd be simpler if she was single. I like my women simple," he added, smirking.

Laurel rolled her eyes. "Your women? Exactly how big is this harem you're inviting me to join?"

"It's only been Pam, these past few months."

"Oh." Her dander settled, and good thing. It was ridiculous to already feel a twinge of jealousy over this man, but it was also an undeniable relief to know she wasn't going to be just one in an endless stable.

"So what about it gets you off, do you think?"

Flynn shrugged, eyes on the road. "Power, I guess."

"Same with the fighting? You like—"

"I'm not real interested in being psychoanalyzed, kiddo. Dissect my rotten soul all you want but keep it to yourself."

"Sorry. I have an engineer's brain."

He side-eyed her. "What's that mean?"

"I like understanding how things work."

"Well, draw yourself a pretty little blueprint and do me a favor and don't ever show it to me. I like fighting, and I like fucking. I don't care much for thinking."

"Okay."

He took a right on Hanover into Laurel's neighborhood. "Tell me where to turn," he said.

"Left on North Bennet."

He drove to her building and put the car in neutral, double-parking on the narrow one-way street. She caught the wink of headlights in the rearview mirror and unstrapped her seat belt. "Thanks for the ride."

"No problem. You got your phone? I'll give you my number, case you need it."

Laurel fished out her cell and he entered his info.

"I never hear it ring, so just leave a message. I'll see you Wednesday at eight," he said, handing her phone back. "If you find the balls."

"I—"

An SUV pulled up behind them and honked. Laurel flung her door open but Flynn grasped her wrist.

"What?"

"Nothing, just makin' that prick wait. I can't fucking stand impatient people."

The horn blared again.

Flynn leaned out his window. "What's the rush at three a.m. on this gorgeous summer evening?" His grip was too tight for Laurel to break.

A series of honks, and Flynn propped his elbow out the window, presumably flipping the driver the bird. Laurel felt her face color. She hated being part of a scene.

"I can wait all night, douchebag," Flynn sang once the horn quieted.

Laurel's heart beat in her throat. A greedy, primitive part of her relished the thought of the pissed-off driver confronting Flynn, only to get loomed over by a tower of black-eyed, split-lipped muscle. Instead they gave a last honk and reversed, fast, turning down a side street with a petulant squeal of tires. Flynn let her hand go and the blood trickled back into her fingertips. She tried to imagine him holding her wrists in another context and blushed deeper, glad it was dark.

"See you Wednesday," she said.

"Up to you."

She got out and slammed the door without looking back. Flynn idled until she'd unlocked the building's front door and closed it behind her. She heard him drive away as she started up the steps, her body mourning the sudden absence of his smell and voice. Wednesday sounded like a hundred years from now.

And Wednesday sounded far too soon.

CHAPTER FOUR

LAUREL STOOD OUTSIDE FLYNN'S BUILDING, sheltering under the awning from the evening's warm rain, staring at the keypad beside a list of tenants. *M. Flynn, 508.* Easy as pie. Just punch in the numbers and buzz his apartment.

She opened her purse and woke her phone. Seven fifty-two. Eight minutes early. Would that look too eager? It wasn't as though she could control how fast the bus got her here… Still, maybe she should take a walk around the block and be fashionably late. Except it was raining and her hair was already fuzzy enough from the humidity—

A knock on the glass in front of her made Laurel yelp and jump. Flynn stood on the other side, staring at her. He made a beckoning motion with his finger as he pushed the locked door open.

"Oh," she said and stepped into the stuffy foyer. "Are you on your way out someplace?"

"No, dipshit, I have an appointment. With you. I saw you walk up the street from my window like five minutes ago. Thought maybe you couldn't figure out the buzzer, Little Miss Engineer."

"Oh," she said again, unable to think of a witty comeback or a good lie. "I was just checking my messages."

"Uh huh. Anyhow, come on up." He turned and she followed him into the elevator.

"Did you have a good day?" she asked.

"Yeah, not bad. You get dinner yet?"

"I did." They exited at the fifth floor and walked down the hall to his apartment. It felt different than when she'd been here on Saturday. More and less intimidating at the same time. Flynn locked up behind them and took her umbrella, hanging it on a hook to drip-dry.

"You tell somebody where you are?" he asked. She'd left him a message the previous afternoon, wanting to double-check his address, and when he called her back he'd told her to do as much.

"I gave my roommate your name and everything," she said.

"Good girl."

Laurel let his patronizing tone slide, pleased he had a clear understanding of how sketchy he was.

She followed him to the living area, finding it looked a little less sinister in the waning daylight, and sober. She turned to Flynn. "So, do we just, you know…get right to it?"

"I'm not a whore," he said, expression somewhere between amused and insulted.

"I didn't mean—"

"Have a seat, sub shop girl. You want a drink? Soda? Wine?" He walked to the counter and held up a bottle of red as Laurel sat on the edge of his couch.

"Yeah, sure. Wine's great."

He uncorked it and poured her a generous measure in a glass with a Christmas holly pattern around the lip. Taking a seat kitty-corner from her on the easy chair, he leaned forward, elbows on his knees.

"So, what are you into?" he asked.

"Sex-wise?"

He nodded.

"I haven't done anything super-crazy before," Laurel said. *Except coming here.*

"Let me know what's off the table. Anal?" he asked, businesslike.

She shrugged. "Not my favorite, but I'll go there. Just, you know…"

"Be gentle?"

She nodded. "That sounds stupid, since I'm here because, you know. You're into rough stuff."

"I don't wanna hurt you. That's the last thing I want. That's why you need to tell me anything you know of that'll freak you out."

"I gag easily," she offered.

"Does it freak you out?"

"No, I wouldn't go that far."

He nodded. "You want condoms with oral?" He seemed to be going down a mental checklist and Laurel wondered how many times he'd conducted this interview.

"Should I, with you?"

"Your choice." He got up and went to a filing cabinet standing between two windows, returning to hand her a paper with hospital letterhead dated three weeks prior—a long list of tests detailing Michael P. Flynn's negative status for all things contagious and undesirable.

Laurel smirked. "Is this what you call foreplay?"

"Pardon me if I kill your buzz, kiddo, but this is important to me. Should be to you too."

"No, it is. Just feels a bit clinical… Anyway I think oral's okay without," she said. "But thanks for offering."

"That doesn't really deserve thanks, but sure. What about you?" he asked. "You clean?"

She nodded, folding the letter and handing it back. "I didn't bring a note though."

"Any traumatic experiences I should avoid triggering? Any off-limits words? You know, the C-word or anything?"

"I don't think so. Just don't call me ugly or anything, please."

He raised an eyebrow. "Any fucker ever tells you that, you give me a call and I'll come over and kick the holy hell out of him for you."

Laurel flushed warmer than she had contemplating any of the other aspects of Flynn's brutality.

"Slapping okay?" he went on. "Like, just spanking to start?"

Her blush ran so deep she could just about taste blood. "Fine."

He nodded again. "All right. We're not gonna get too crazy tonight, but if anything feels off to you, just use my first name and we'll stop. You remember my first name?"

"Michael," she said. He couldn't possibly guess how many times she'd repeated it in her mind in the last four days.

"Good. And so you know, there's no hidden cameras or any of that shit. And you're welcome to look for yourself," he said. "For what I am, I'm a decent guy. I don't want you here if you don't think you believe that yet."

"I trust you."

"How do you want it to end tonight?"

"What do you mean?" she asked.

"Unless you tell me not to, I'm gonna come, for one. I'll try to make you come too if you want me to. But if you think you'd rather leave hot and frustrated, I can do that."

"I wouldn't mind coming." She raised the glass to her lips to hide a nervous smile.

"You got it. And what about afterward? You want to get tossed out on your ass? You want a lift home? You can stay the night, but I don't cuddle or spoon and I leave at a quarter to six for work."

"Do I have to decide now?"

He shook his head. "Nope. Only if you want this to end with me acting like a jerk and giving you the boot."

"Is that what girls usually want you to do?"

"No, not usually. But it's an option."

"And what…what do you need from me?"

He made a face then laughed. "Don't think a woman's ever asked me that before. And I guess I just need you to be here with good intentions. Don't make me live the rest of my life feelin' shitty about anything I do to you that you didn't warn me not to. That's about it."

"I'll try not to."

"Good. And I'll tell you now, I won't be callin' you tomorrow or the next day or the day after that, so don't get in a stink when I don't. None of the normal dating rules apply to this. I know what goes on here is twisted as fuck as far as most people are concerned, and I don't want to be the creepy fucker callin' up some girl he accidentally freaked out. If you decide you want to do this again, you call me. You decide I'm a jerk, don't. My feelings won't be hurt."

"Okay." Laurel took a deep drink and grimaced at the sour wine.

A smile melted Flynn's stern, professional expression. "Sorry. I'm useless with booze. I just picked the one with the girliest label."

"Are you…" She trailed off.

"Recovering?"

She nodded.

"Nah. I just don't drink. Not since I was like twenty-five. Just a glass of something at a wedding or whatever. You remember what I said about coffee?"

"Yeah."

"Yeah. I'm twitchy enough without chemicals short-circuitin' shit in my head."

"Maybe you should take up smoking," Laurel teased.

He stood. "Don't fuckin' tempt me. Hardest breakup of my life, me and cigarettes."

"How long were you going out?"

Flynn looked at the ceiling, doing math in his head. "Twelve years." He went to the sink to fill a pint glass with water.

"Wow, well done." Laurel raised her own glass and choked down another gulp in honor of Flynn's abstinence. Gut-rotting or not, the wine was working. She felt heat creeping over her skin, loosening her muscles and mouth and inhibitions.

"Can you tell I'm super-nervous?" she asked.

He seemed to study her face. "I'd be worried if you weren't. But no, you don't seem that nervous."

"Are *you* nervous?"

"Nah." He sat back down with his glass. "I've been on board with this part of myself for a few years now, and I know when a girl's worth gettin' nervous over."

Laurel frowned, insulted. "What do you mean?"

"You didn't show up with a trench coat, so I know you're not going to whip it off and be wearin' some crazy get-up made out of black plastic and dog collars, askin' me to parade you down Broadway."

"Oh. But you're not nervous about, I don't know…your performance or whatever?"

"Should I be? You got high standards?"

She considered it a moment and Flynn laughed.

"Neither of us is here to prove anything," he said. "We're here to have fun, and for you to maybe get your motor cranked like you never knew it could be. Or not. Who knows? My ego's not tied up in this going a certain way. The only thing that makes me nervous is hurtin' you by mistake, and I trust myself enough to think that's unlikely."

"Are you good about knowing? You know, if a woman's about to freak out."

He nodded. "I think fighting's taught me how to read people pretty good."

"You should take up poker." Laurel drained her glass and set it aside. "Do you have some kind of waiver I should sign, Mr. Preparedness?"

"Nah, let's start. If I do something that makes you want to sue me, I'll probably deserve it."

Laurel smiled at him, feeling as if she'd uncovered a complex new dimension of a man who'd seemed so simple at first glance. He really stuck his neck out for this, putting his faith in his partners as much as they did him. Maybe more.

"You're really quite…trusting," Laurel offered.

"And you're really quite attractive when you bust my balls, sub shop girl. Why don't we get down to business and see how this goes?"

The chatting and alcohol had eased the tension in Laurel's body but it flooded back with a vengeance as Flynn sat beside her. His weight shifted the couch cushions, reminding her just how big he was.

She cleared her throat. "Can we keep it pretty vanilla, to start? And I could tell you when I might want you to get…meaner?"

He nodded. "Whatever you need."

"Okay, good." She studied his eyes, different than she remembered. Blue with a dark outer ring and a burst of amber around the pupil. She realized she probably looked silly, her own eyes crossed from staring at him this close up.

Then he kissed her, and she couldn't give a good goddamn about anything except his mouth.

Training wheels or not, Flynn only gave her a couple soft kisses before his tongue slid between her lips, hot and slick and aggressive. She sucked a breath through her nose, focusing on her body's thrill and filtering out the fear.

His palms felt broad and warm as they grazed her neck, a little taste of the promised roughness in the way his fingers tangled in her hair, freeing half of it from the elastic. She stroked his shoulders and chest, taking in those firm contours as his tongue delved deeper.

He pulled away to say, "Get on my lap."

A shiver trickled through her at that first order. She toyed with saying "Yes, Sir," but wasn't ready to dive into the submissive role quite so soon.

She tossed a leg over and straddled him. Flynn's eyes and hands roamed her sides, her arms, her small breasts. She touched his face and hair and ears then he grabbed one of her hands and put it to his mouth, sliding two fingers between his lips. He sucked hard, making her fingertips prickle and her eyes widen. She felt his tongue push between the digits, then the drag of his teeth down her skin. He made a throaty noise that raised the hairs along her arms and he pulled her fingers out.

"Take your top off," he said.

Her body warmed at being commanded by this man. She'd done little snatches of role-playing with lovers but it'd always felt cheesy and awkward. Not with Flynn. She knew he wasn't play-acting. She peeled her shirt up and tossed it over the arm of the couch.

"Nice," he whispered, eyes darting over her skin. His rough palms swept up her stomach and ribs, cupped her breasts. "Didn't anybody tell you it's July?" He meant her pale skin.

"I'm not really a beach person." She glanced down at her freckled arms and the white skin of her trunk that never saw the sun.

"I like it," he said, still staring. "You must be Irish."

"I'm a mutt. And don't forget the red hair's not really mine."

He ignored her attempt at self-deprecation. Reaching around, he got her bra clasp open. Another husky, appreciative noise escaped him as the garment dropped. His touch started light, the graze of his fingers stiffening her nipples. He cupped her breasts, squeezing and kneading softly, then a bit rougher. Laurel got her first taste of physical dominance when his palm slid to her lower back, jerking her closer, higher. She braced a hand on the couch. His lips claimed one breast as he palmed the other, and her free hand went instinctively to the back of his head, nails raking his scalp.

Hard suction, then a glancing of teeth.

"God." It came out as barely more than a grunt.

He freed his mouth. "Say my name."

"Flynn."

A smug noise warmed her wet skin. "Keep saying it. It gets me so fuckin' hard."

Fever burned in her neck and cheeks as she thought of arousing him and she shifted her hips, wanting to feel the evidence. Pressing their centers close, she ground against the stiff ridge hiding behind his fly. "Flynn."

"Yeah." His mouth moved to her other breast, even rougher than with the first. His thick thighs fidgeted between hers, his swelling cock craving more space or more friction as the tension mounted.

"You feel big," Laurel whispered.

He pulled his head away. "You wanna see me?"

She nodded.

"Push that table back and get on your knees."

She got off his lap, slid the coffee table away and knelt between his feet. Her heart raced, a hundred percent excitement, zero fear.

Flynn scooted forward so his thighs flanked her ribs. He tugged off his shirt, offering the spectacle of all that powerful muscle, the smell of his skin.

Laurel didn't wait for an order. She reached for his belt, getting the buckle open and letting the worn, heavy leather fall aside. She freed the button and lowered his zipper, then spread his jeans open, revealing a strip of black cotton. She caught the first hint of his scent, one that made her mouth prickle in anticipation. He eased his jeans down a couple more inches and adjusted his cock, centering the impressive bulge in his open fly.

She glanced up to meet his eyes, wanting an order this time.

"Touch it." Cold.

Laurel swallowed and put her fingertips to the ridge, feeling his flesh react. She flattened her palm, surveyed his broad, fevered erection, reveled in his sharp inhalation. His hand covered hers, wrapping it tight around him, making her feel how thick and hard and ready he'd grown.

He moaned above her. "Yeah... Fuck, I've been thinking about this all week, making you touch my cock. Get it out, girl."

She tugged his waistband down, exposing every throbbing inch, wrapping her hand around him again and loving the smooth feel of his skin.

"Good girl." His hips flexed into her slow, gentle exploration. "Harder." He guided her hand again, tightening her grip and quickening her stroke. "That's good. That's good. I want this so bad." He made their shared rhythm fast and rough and groaned in time with the pulls. "I've been jerking off thinking about this. About making you taste me." Pre-come beaded at his slit then slid down his head to ease the motions.

"Flynn."

"I'm so fucking ready, you're gonna get me off before we even start playing. Taste me," he ordered.

Laurel brought her mouth to him as their hands continued to work. She kissed his head, gave him a light lick.

"Yeah. More. Tongue me."

She lapped at his slit, lavishing it with wet caresses.

"Good girl. Tease it. Tease it and I'll reward you with a nice mouthful."

Her face burned as she took his orders, the sounds of his panting breaths and the salty taste of him leaving her lightheaded. She flicked her tongue over him, savoring a flash of power as his bossy hand faltered and his grunts turned to shallow gasps.

"God, fuck." He tangled his fingers in her hair, holding her head but not forcing her mouth. Not yet. "Keep it tight," he said, and she squeezed him harder. "Keep teasing me."

She fluttered her tongue across his slit, the taste of his pre-come greeting her in steady bursts. She neglected him just long enough to say, "You taste so good."

"Yeah. Take more of me. Suck my cock."

Bitch, she added to herself, the word seeming implicit from his harsh tone. She took him into her mouth, sucking hard. Any discomfort was worth it just for the sounds he made.

"More. Nice and deep."

She worked her mouth lower, letting his head bump the back of her throat and trigger her gag reflex. It didn't ease as she bobbed her head, but the sensation only heightened the experience, the taboo.

"All of it," Flynn ordered, starting to force her. Though he was rough, he knew what he was doing. His demanding hands made her swallow every inch but he withdrew with each protest from her throat, gave her a chance to find her breath. He pulled out after a minute and got to his feet, making Laurel shuffle back on the hard floor. He brought his cock back to her lips, adding his own thrusts and showing her the deep rhythm he craved.

"I love it," he whispered. "I love fucking that sweet mouth of yours." His hips sped for a few beats, emphasizing, overwhelming Laurel for a breath or two before he settled into a manageable pace.

"You're so good at sucking that cock, girl." He traced her lips with his thumb. "I'm gonna reward you. You want that?"

She moaned an affirmation around his shaft. He pulled her hair, yanking her head back and holding it at arm's length. "Jerk me. Hard as you fucking can."

She wrapped her hand around his slick cock and stroked so aggressively she feared she'd hurt him.

"Good. Keep going. Keep that up."

A desperate, needy feeling clouded her mind as he held her hair, keeping her mouth just out of reach of his crown. She jerked him until she could see his hips and abs trembling, his breath racing from her mean strokes.

"You're gonna get it," he rasped. "You're gonna get a big fuckin' mouthful of me." He groaned, the sound reverberating in Laurel's bones. His free hand pushed hers away, taking over the pulls as the other brought her head close, forcing his cock past her lips as he released. His stroking fist bumped her chin as the come lashed her tongue, a long, hot stream of him bathing her taste buds and sliding down her throat. The roughness of his commands blended with the helpless sound of his moan, making Laurel feel in control for the briefest of moments.

He released her as his body stilled.

"Clean me up," he said, panting.

Laurel reached out and took his softening cock, laving it until he stepped away. She watched him walk to the sink and fill a glass from the tap. She looked to her top and her bra slung over the couch and wondered with a stab of panic if the evening's activities were already over—if she was supposed to be getting dressed and making a decision about whether or not she was staying. Flynn set his glass on the counter and turned to face her.

"Okay. We've got about twenty minutes before I get mean again."

CHAPTER FIVE

LAUREL LAUGHED, relieved the night was still young. "What are you, some kind of sex-werewolf?"

He let out a heavy sigh, blinked a couple times and walked over, zipping his jeans and buckling his belt. "Here," he said, putting out a hand. "Get up. Looks weird havin' a topless girl on my floor when I'm not in barbarian mode."

He helped her to standing and she dusted off her knees. "So. What do we do for twenty minutes?"

His hands went to Laurel's jeans, undoing her button and zipper. She giggled.

He looked up. "What?"

"Sorry. I can't get over how big your fingers are."

He stared at them a moment.

"Not just your fingers, I mean. All of you." She looked to his eyes, probably eight or nine inches above hers, and she wasn't particularly short. "How tall are you?"

"Six-three-and-a-half."

"Damn."

He shrugged and turned back to her jeans, pushing them down her hips. He sucked in a soft breath.

It was her turn to ask, "What?"

"I dunno. Just your skin. You're so…white."

"One of my roommates calls me Ghostie."

He shook his head. "You're like that famous chick, what's her name?"

Laurel knew exactly what name he was looking for but refused to supply it. Pale skin and red hair, but she lacked Nicole Kidman's height and bone structure and glamour and didn't feel like hearing their differences enumerated if Flynn made a project of comparing them.

"So what do we do now?" she asked again.

"You get in my bed and I figure a few things out about you before the beast returns. If you're still in the mood."

She kicked off her jeans with gusto and jogged to toss herself across his rumpled comforter. She listened to his laugh as she stared into the maze of pipes and vents traversing the ceiling, anticipating. His footsteps faded and the lights went out. More steps, and a dim reading lamp clamped to one of the bedside shelves flipped on. Flynn sat on the mattress, the heaviness of him thrilling Laurel deep down to her marrow.

"Lie on your side," he said. "Away from me."

She complied and he slid up behind her, pressing his bare chest into her back, pushing a hard thigh between her knees. He ran his warm palm up and down her hip and made a soft noise, a whisper crossed with a grunt. His hand slid up her ribs to cup her breast, the sensation tightening her legs around his.

"I wanna know what you like," he said.

She realized that with his mouth this close and his tone hushed, the voice she'd found brash and a bit grating was actually rather sexy.

She cleared her throat. "Well, I'm here because I want to see what it's like to be with someone, you know…like you."

"Have you thought about it? Since the last time you were here?" His fingers pinched her nipple gently, then meaner.

"Yeah, I've thought about it. A lot." She'd gotten off about ten times in the last four days, imagining fucking Flynn. No, not fucking Flynn—being fucked *by* Flynn.

His hand moved down her belly to rest on her mound. "Tell me."

Laurel hesitated. She'd always been lousy at dirty talk.

"Listen, kiddo," he said. "I'm a selfish prick, and I want to be the greatest fuck of your life and ruin you for every man who comes after me. But I'm not a mind reader, so I need some help. Otherwise I could end up as the douchebag who's got shitty taste in wine and totally traumatized you when you were thirty."

"Twenty-nine."

"So tell me," he breathed, right behind her ear. "What do you want me to do to you?"

She took a deep breath, held it as his hand slid low, two fingers just barely pressing into her lips through her underwear. "I thought about everything you did with her. And wondered what it'd be like to do that with you."

"What else?" Those fingers ran up and down her crease, flooding her sex with heat and pressure.

Confession became far easier.

"I thought about you making me get on my elbows and knees, on your floor, like you did to her."

"Uh huh." His touch intensified, his thigh pushing her knees wider as his fingers strained against the cotton.

"Except you tie my wrists," she said. "And instead of telling me to keep my eyes on the floor, there's, like, a mirror against the wall in front of me, so I have to watch you while you fuck me." Her throat was tight, as tight as her pussy under his touch.

"And how do I fuck you?" he asked, voice turning harsh, hand slipping beneath her panties, tickling her hair before his fingers found her folds and banished all other thoughts and sensations. She moaned.

"Tell me how I fuck you."

"Hard," she managed. "And mean."

"Am I forcing you?" Two fingers penetrated.

"Oh God."

"Tell me. Do you want me to force you?" He pushed deeper.

"Yeah," she said, barely able to form the syllable as he began to thrust.

"You're so wet," he whispered, sounding smug. "I can't wait to ram my cock inside you. See your hot body below me as I take you."

He fucked her fast, his slick fingers curled into a hook, the pad of his hand stroking her clit each time he withdrew. Against her ass she felt him growing hard. The buckle of his belt made her think of her hands bound again, fueling the fire. She groaned on each exhale, drunk from his touch and his smell, his voice. He was turning back into the other Flynn, just as he'd promised.

"You like that, don't you?" She could hear his sneer. "Bet you wish that was my cock, don't you?" His fingers fucked her hard for half a minute and she writhed against him, desperate. "You sucked me so good before. I loved watching you take every inch."

"God, Flynn."

His dick was stiff, as hard as it had been when she'd sucked him.

"You'll say my name just like that when I make you come, bitch."

Her breath hitched at the word but the intimidation wasn't unwelcome.

"You want to live out that fantasy tonight?" His hips pumped, rubbing his erection against her bottom.

"I'm not sure."

"We can do the training wheels version."

She gasped when he pulled away, turned her onto her back and knelt between her thighs, spreading them wide and bringing his groin to hers.

"I love your fantasy." He stared down at her, fire in his eyes. He thrust his cock against her, the layers of fabric taunting. "I wanna watch you in that mirror, watching me. Close your eyes and think about it."

She obeyed. His cock rubbed her pussy with hot, frustrating friction. Flynn's face was fresh in her mind, that cruel smile, dark expression. Plus his bare body with all those strong muscles, flexing with each thrust...

She opened her eyes. "I want that."

"Good." He changed, suddenly businesslike. His hips stilled and he wedged a knee under hers to kneel wide before her, put a hand on each of her shins. "We're gonna keep things pretty tame tonight. I won't actually tie your hands, but you're gonna pretend I do. And you're gonna set the tone. You think you want to pretend I'm forcing you, you make it clear and I'll play along. Okay?"

She nodded.

He slapped her calf. "Go make a trip to the ladies' room if you need one, and I'll get things set up. When you come back it's game-on."

"Okay."

"What's your safe word?"

"Michael."

He slapped her calf again. "Good girl. And if for some reason you can't say it and you need to, you grunt three times, fast, or hit your foot or your hand against something, three times. Got it?"

She nodded again.

He got his legs out from under hers and stood beside the bed. "Bring me back a towel. A big one."

Laurel grabbed her purse and went to the bathroom, tidying her makeup for a couple minutes, the whirring fan drowning out whatever Flynn might be doing in the other room. When she emerged with a bath towel he was crouched by the open closet near the bed, a toolbox by his foot. He unscrewed the bottom of a full-length mirror from the door then stood and detached the top. He walked it to a bare stretch of wall and leaned it there. He took the towel from Laurel and lay it on the floor, clearly thinking her getting her knees and elbows savaged by the not-so-recently swept hardwood was too varsity for her first night.

Flynn straightened and the cold look on his face said the fantasy had begun. A chill trickled down Laurel's spine as she stared into his narrowed eyes.

"Sit on the bed," he said.

She hesitated—only for a second but it was enough to earn some correction. Flynn took her by the shoulders and forced her back a couple steps, pushing her onto the edge of the mattress beside a pair of wrapped condoms, a bottle of lube and a roll of duct tape. Being physically controlled by someone she knew she couldn't ever hope to fight off was both arousing and terrifying. This man could *actually* rape her, if he was so inclined—he was physically capable of it. She felt her throat constrict as if a fist had closed around it.

"M-Michael."

His posture transformed in an instant. He sat down next to her on the bed, hands clasped between his knees, wary eyes on her face. "Too rough?"

She gulped a breath. "I'm not sure. I think mostly I just wanted to test the safe word. I think I needed to know you'd stop, if I asked you to."

"Always."

Then Laurel did something that surprised even herself. She turned and put her palm to his jaw. She brought her face up and drew his

65

down and kissed his mouth. A first-date, good-night kiss. No tongue, just lips finding their way for a few moments. His hand settled on her arm, patient and reassuring.

Laurel pulled away feeling safe, knowing she was calling the shots. Her relief morphed to curiosity as she stared at his naked chest and arms. Fuck, those arms.

"I'm ready," she decided aloud. "You can do whatever you were planning on." She squared her shoulders and looked expectant, as if he'd just pushed her down onto the bed. He licked his lips and nodded, seeming satisfied that she was back on board. He stood and put his knees between hers, a hand coming down to hold the back of her head.

"Take me out and get me hard." Laurel's new favorite order.

She undid his belt and fly, let his jeans drop to the ground. Cupping his bulge, she rubbed her thumbs across his ridge, feeling him go stiff. She stroked her hand up and down his length as he grew, measuring and anticipating.

A tiny pang of sadness struck, as she realized that the first time he penetrated her they wouldn't be face-to-face. She'd miss out on that cautious, awe-filled, one-time-only moment between new lovers with this man.

Flynn eased his waistband over his straining cock and pushed his shorts down his thighs. His hand wrapped around hers as before, gripping to dictate her strokes.

"Yeah, good." The weight returned to his voice. "Make it nice and big." He wound her hair around his other hand, possessive.

"What are you going to do?" she asked, eyes on his swollen head above their two fists.

"Depends on if you cooperate or not. You gonna get on your hands and knees for me, girl?"

She glanced at the duct tape then nodded.

He let her go after a couple more strokes and she got to the ground, all fours on the towel, facing the mirror. Flynn kicked his pants and shorts away and grabbed the tape, kneeling behind her.

"Sit up," he said.

She sat back on her haunches. She heard the rip of tape being yanked and detached, glanced over her shoulder to watch him folding the three-foot length in half the long way, closing the sticky side in on itself. He reached around her waist to press her wrists together, wrapping them with the tape, tucking the ends beneath her thumbs so the only things keeping her bound were her own fists. Staring down at her hands, Laurel thought it looked pretty damn convincing.

"Back on all fours."

She settled on her knees and elbows, keeping the bindings tight. Strong hands yanked her underwear down her thighs and out from under her knees. A hungry noise rattled out of Flynn's chest, the closest thing to a growl Laurel had ever heard a man make.

She watched his face in the mirror, his eyes cast down at her ass or her pussy, his ready cock just inches away. He reached for a condom, unwrapped it. As he rolled it on his other hand fucked her, fingers thrusting into her wet folds. She pushed her hips eagerly into the touch, watching his roped arms in the mirror, his flexing belly and tight chest. She'd never really prioritized a guy's physique when choosing a lover before, but right now Laurel wished the whole world could see this man. Powerful—that was the only word for him. Then his eyes caught hers in the reflection and she forgot all about his body.

"Beg me," he said, holding her gaze.

"Please, Flynn."

"Please what?" He let his dick rest along the cleft of her ass as he grabbed her hip. He tugged her hard onto his fingers as his cock slid along her crack, balls bumping her. His fucking hand reached around to spear her from the front.

"Fuck me, Flynn. Please. I want you so bad."

"I know you do. I can feel it." The hand on her hip rose to come down with a slap. "You're so tight and hot for me."

"Please."

"Or maybe you mean something else," he said. His hips drew back and his fingers left her pussy. She felt them fan across her butt, his thumb slipping into her crack. The wet pad teased her hole. Trepidation tightened her body but with Flynn in control the nerves felt right. She gave herself over to whatever he wanted, trusting he'd sense her boundaries.

His patient voice returned for a moment. "Breathe, sweetheart."

She exhaled, pushing the anxiety out of her lungs. His thumb rubbed in a tight circle.

"Again," he said.

She pushed out another deep breath and he pressed his thumb inside. Laurel swallowed and winced, accepting the violation, trying to welcome the sensation. Still not her favorite thing, but with Flynn she didn't feel pressured or coerced, cajoled. He was simply *dirty*, ready to take, seemingly without permission. For some odd reason it made Laurel trust him more than any boyfriend who'd ever tried to win her over by detailing the many spurious feminist virtues of taking it up the ass.

"Good." He pushed his thumb in a little deeper, gave her a few slow, short thrusts. "Good. We'll get you there sometime, but probably not too soon. Not 'til you're begging me for it."

A wave of relief engulfed her as he eased his thumb out and took hold of her hip. She felt the tip of his cock tease her lips.

"Please, Flynn."

She watched his reflection. His mouth was open, eyes on the juncture of their bodies. His broad chest rose and fell, deep and steady. He pushed in, the penetration explicit in its slowness.

Laurel moaned. "Oh God."

He was big, seeming even bigger now that his matching frame wasn't distorting the scale of things. In the mirror his entire body looked tight and strained, his face harsh. He eased in another inch, the thick, powerful feel of him making Laurel drunk.

"Fuck, you're tight."

"More," she whispered.

He grunted, pushed, gave her another couple inches.

"Don't stop, Flynn."

"Yeah." He eased out, pushed back in, over and over until he had her filled. As good as his arms and abs looked in the mirror, she wished she could see his cock, his ass, his back muscles. He gave a few long thrusts, all the way in, nearly all the way out, making her feel every slick, hard inch as it slid deep and withdrew.

"Tight and deep," he said through a labored breath. He sped up, setting an even pace, hands stroking her ass and thighs as his hips found their rhythm.

She craned her neck to meet his eyes, unreflected. "Flynn."

"God, I love your cunt. You're so fuckin' hot." One hand left her flank to reach around and tease her pussy and he brought his thumb back to her ass, slick. He slid it inside, rougher than before, the feeling intensified tenfold by the thrust of his cock.

"Oh God."

"That's right." He pushed the digit in deep and kept it there as his cock pounded. "I'd fuck your mouth too, if I could."

Laurel turned back to the mirror, adrenaline whirling through her body, making her feel crazed and unafraid. She clenched her thumbs tight around the tape and thrashed her hips.

Flynn missed a beat but started right back up, harder than before. "You keep still."

Laurel moved again, walking a knee forward only to get yanked back.

"I said don't fucking move," he warned, cold eyes trained on her face in the mirror.

She let the feelings crash over her, fear and excitement heating her from the inside out, the chemical rush in her brain compounding it all, getting her high. She struggled again, this time trying to break away for real, needing to feel how easy it was for him to stop her. Both his hands shot forward as he leaned over her, grabbed her behind the elbows and folded her arms up beneath her, her shoulders and head coming down, chin landing just above her bound fists with a soft thump against the towel. He pushed down on her back, pinning her as the fucking turned harsh, each impact punctuated by the slap of his damp skin against hers. Laurel turned her head, willing to put up with the uncomfortable position if it meant she could see his face. She saw control in his eyes, cool beside the hot flush of his skin.

"Don't," she whispered.

"Shut up."

She moved the only bit of herself she had power over—her legs.

"Don't make this hard," he warned, keeping her in place with his weight.

She gave a desperate thrash and his hands left her back. He shoved her knees together and widened his stance, clamping his thighs beside hers and locking them. She had a second to put up a fight with her bound arms before he pinned them down again.

"Now you're gonna get it," he said.

Laurel made a fearful, breathy noise and was rewarded with a few violent thrusts. "Stop," she panted. "Please."

"I said shut up."

"Please, stop."

"Fine. Gets me hot when you beg, anyway."

She alternated pleading with helpless noises, the role-playing arousing her more than she'd imagined possible. Flynn felt godlike behind her, insanely strong and powerful. His dick drove deep, over and over, the heat built with every excruciating minute, sweat making their skin slippery, exertion changing his breathing and voice and rhythm.

"God, yeah. I can't wait to shoot in you, bitch."

Laurel sensed him getting close. Her own body was as tight as she'd ever been without touching herself. The sensation was maddening but ecstatic and the second he let her go she was going to get a hand free and tease herself over the edge.

She made a couple useless attempts at struggling, too excited by his arousal now to put on a good show. One of Flynn's hands left her back, his damp palm sliding across her stomach, fingers finding her clit. She bucked and yelped at the contact.

"Yeah, that's right. I knew you loved it." He fucked her fast, rubbed her clit and drew all the heat of her body into a pounding, swirling mass against the pads of his fingers.

"God, Flynn."

"Good. Come for me. Come all over that big dick I'm fucking you with."

She groaned as the climax rose, the sweet burn tingling up her thighs and bursting open against his fingers, around his cock.

"Yeah, yeah, yeah." He pounded her deep and fast as the orgasm tossed her, teased her clit lighter and lighter as her cries died away.

"Good girl."

To her surprise, he let her go. His thrusts stopped and his hands left her. He stood. "Can you get up?"

Laurel oozed out a delirious breath and rocked back onto her knees, registering the crick in her neck and the blood pooling in her fingers. She opened her hands and the tape fell away. Flynn helped her to her feet and she looked to him for instruction.

"Wanna lie down? On the bed?"

"Sure." She sat on the mattress and shimmied herself into the center on her back. Flynn climbed on after her and got his knees between hers.

"Feel okay? Not too roughed up for me to finish?"

"Oh," she said, "you better fucking finish."

His brows rose. "Guess that's a yes."

"I want to see you come," she said, all the urgent desire from before her climax bubbling right back up.

Flynn angled his cock between her thighs and she watched as he drove inside, slow, filling her.

"God, you're big."

"That what you like?" he asked, starting to fuck.

"I guess I do." She reached down to circle her thumb and finger around him, squeezing to feel how stiff and thick he was. "And you're so hard."

"You can have this big, hard cock anytime you want," he promised, hips hammering fast. "Say my name."

She did. She said it again and again as he drove himself to the edge. She took in the strong arms locked at her side, his slick chest, his face as he lost control.

"Fuck, yeah." He yanked himself out, leaning back to strip off the condom and jerk himself home with a rough fist. He came hard with a strangled noise, come lashing her belly in warm ribbons until the aggression waned, fading like a plume of smoke.

"Fuck." He composed himself a moment, panting, then left the bed to grab the towel so he could wipe Laurel's skin. He tossed it aside and collapsed onto his back next to her.

She listened to his racing breaths. "Wow."

Flynn laughed, the sound turning into a brief coughing fit. He cleared his throat. "Yeah," he said. "Wow." He folded his arms under his head and Laurel did the same and they both stared up at the vents.

At length, she turned to study his face. "So I did okay for my inaugural night?"

He returned the scrutiny. "Yeah, that was fantastic. You liked it then?"

She nodded.

"Good. I hope you'll give me a call sometime."

Laurel decided she rather liked Flynn's unambiguous style of flirting. "And what you said before—it's still okay if I crash here? My legs feel like their bones fell out."

"Sure. Just be prepared to get up real early. I can run you back home before I start work."

"You can just dump me at the nearest T stop."

"You live ten minutes' drive from my site, dummy. I'm not making you take the subway. Damn thing's always derailing and catching fire anyhow."

"Fine then." She yawned deeply. It was probably only nine but she felt as if she'd been up all night. "I don't suppose I could borrow a T-shirt to sleep in?"

"Course. Just gimme a minute to recover."

She studied his face. "You know, you're really a very nice man."

He laughed. "That orgasm must have fucked you up in the head."

Laurel smiled. She was mindful to obey his non-cuddling rule but inched her top half over a little so their shoulders touched. She felt sleep drawing its cloudy veil over her brain. "Thanks."

"What for?"

"The fucking," she said through a yawn.

"You're welcome."

She closed her eyes and breathed him in, the musky smell of their sex and the subtler ones of his apartment and sheets. "I'm definitely going to call you," she murmured.

"Good. I hope you do."

"Definitely," she said again, dreamy. She felt Flynn leave the bed, heard a drawer scrape open, then cool cotton flopped over her arm and breast.

"I'm gonna take a shower," he said. "Looks like you'll be out cold when I get back."

"I wouldn't put it past me."

He wandered off and Laurel heard the fan kick on in the bathroom. She managed to fumble into the shirt and under his covers. His sheets smelled of him, and *Christ* it was heavenly. She had just enough clarity leftover to think of something that intimidated her more than anything else Flynn had offered tonight.

I like him.

She liked him enough that knowing he could be with another woman tomorrow would sting if she let it.

But right now, he was hers. Until he dropped her at her door the next morning, she was the only one who got him. She smiled into one of his threadbare pillowcases and let the smug comfort of the thought carry her into sleep.

Tonight he was hers. Tomorrow could go fuck itself.

CHAPTER SIX

"HEY. SUB SHOP GIRL."

Laurel opened her eyes to find Flynn standing beside the bed, dressed.

"Rise and shine, kiddo."

"What time is it?"

"Five ten," he said. "You got time for a quick shower if you need one."

"Can I use that time to sleep?"

"Sure."

Flynn wandered away and Laurel buried her head deeper in the pillow, but she didn't sleep. Her pulse spiked as she registered what they'd done last night. Then it slowed as she realized there didn't seem to be any reason to panic.

After a minute she tossed the covers aside and sat on the edge of his bed, looking around Flynn's apartment. It was dark, just the light above the stove switched on. The city beyond the windows looked purple and sleepy, sunrise hidden by a hundred tall buildings to the east.

Flynn was on the couch, lacing his boots. Laurel padded to the coffee table to grab her purse. She caught Flynn's eyes dart to her breasts in the tee she'd borrowed then a glance at where its hem brushed her upper thigh. She smirked at him.

He smiled and went back to his laces and Laurel closed herself in the bathroom.

She scrubbed her face and freshened her makeup, finger-combed her tangled hair and thought its messiness looked rather fashionable. She dug out her travel toothbrush and got her mouth in order, lifted up the shirt to check for any marks on her body and didn't find any. She pouted, a bit sad about that.

Her clothes were still slung over the easy chair, including the panties she'd lost on the floor by the bed. She cast Flynn a glance before stripping off the shirt, pleased by his rapt expression as he watched her, his hands clasped politely between his knees.

"Subtle," she teased, adjusting her bra.

"You sleep okay?"

"Yup." She pulled her tank top on then her jeans. "Very roomy in that bed." She sat down across from him and slipped on her flats. "Okay. I'm ready."

Flynn went to his dresser, found a checked button-up and slipped it on over his tee shirt, grabbed his key ring off the counter and clipped it to his belt. Laurel followed him out. She stole glances at his face as they rode the elevator down, looking for signs of awkwardness or regret, but he was tough to read. He unlocked her side of the station wagon first then dropped into the driver's seat.

"Thanks for the lift," she said, feeling suddenly shy.

"Thanks for the hot sex," Flynn replied, paused a moment, then grinned at her. He flipped his headlights on and started the engine.

"You too."

"Still not traumatized?"

"I don't seem to be."

"Good."

Laurel stared out her window as he steered them down the near-empty streets of South Boston, thinking it was a strange time of day, lit like dusk but with none of its energy.

She turned to him as they drove over the first bridge. "Can I ask you a question?"

"You just did."

"Have you always known that's how you are? Like, in bed?"

"No."

"When did you figure it out?" she asked.

"Well," he said, "maybe I sort of knew, when I was younger. But I wasn't one of those guys who was into that kind of stuff."

"What kind of stuff?"

"You know, like if those fucked-up *Saw* movies had been out when I was a teenager, or websites with creepy-ass rape fantasy shit on them, I don't think I would've been into it. I sort of knew what turned my crank, but I didn't like that it did. Call it Catholic guilt, maybe. Plus like I said, it's not a fetish. Less rough stuff can get me off, so I sort of shoved it away in the back of my skull."

"Until?"

"Until I was about twenty-two, and I was dating this girl, and one night she asked me to boss her around and hold her down." Flynn stopped to let a woman cross the road with her dog. "And I dunno, it was like a switch got flipped. Like a switch attached to my dick flipped on and I fucking caught fire."

"Wow."

"Yeah. I didn't know anything about safe words or any of the rules people use when they're into D/s stuff, and eventually I think I just freaked her out, asking way too often if we could do that again. It totally took over the relationship and she dumped me and said I was a sick-o and a sex fiend and to go fuck myself. Which was fair. I can see how being too eager about wanting to pretend-rape your girlfriend could be creepy as fuck."

Laurel nodded.

"That wasn't, like, an epic breakup. I mean, we'd been going out for a couple months. But she demonized me enough that I got insecure about how things ended and I shoved it all down again, worried I was some kinda latent rapist."

"When did you get all well-adjusted with it?"

Flynn pushed a breath through his nose, expression thoughtful. "When I was twenty-six, I think it was. I started seeing this woman— not dating, just sort of friendly sex. Kinda like with you."

That gave Laurel a warm little jolt. To hear that the two of them were *something*.

"She came with another guy to the fights one night," Flynn went on, "and she saw whatever it is about me, and I got to her, I guess. So she approached me after a couple weeks and we started hanging out and messing around. She was a couple years older than me and about ten years smarter about sex, and she was the first woman who ever asked me, 'So what are you into?' And I was honest, for the first time. And she was into it, and she sort of set me straight about how rough stuff is supposed to work."

"Ah." Laurel tried to ignore the knot of jealousy tightening in her gut. "How long did that go on for?"

"It was kind of random, like we'd hang out every week or two, for quite a while. Six months, maybe."

"Why did it end, do you think?" she asked.

"She moved to San Francisco."

"Oh. That'd do it." Laurel stared out the window, wondering what this mystery sex goddess looked like. "Were you in love with her?"

He didn't answer immediately. "I thought I was. Not while we were hooking up, but when I found out she was leaving I was pretty upset. I thought she was the only woman on Earth I'd ever find who'd let me be how I wanted in bed, and it felt like something monumental was being taken away. But I mean, I didn't try to follow her or anything. And eventually I learned that those magic words— what are you into?—are all you really need. You just keep askin' people that and eventually you find someone who fits with you." He looked at her pointedly.

"Yeah," Laurel said. "Or maybe you don't know you're into something but then you stalk some stranger all through the Financial District until he gives you the address to his shady underground boxing syndicate."

"I hear that works too. Anyhow, I'm at a point now where I know what I like, and I can admit it's a deal-breaker if a woman I'm getting to know isn't into it." He stopped at a red light. "I'd rather go without and be lonely than not be how I really want with someone."

She felt a laugh bubble up but turned it into a huff. "You get lonely?"

He glowered at her a moment before it melted into a smile. "Course I do. I don't drink, so I don't get shitfaced and start cryin' and singin' with my drunk-ass guy friends. Sex is... I dunno, it's, like, the realest sort of human experience I got, aside from fighting. It's hard, going without. I got nothin' against sitting up 'til one a.m. playing canasta with my sister, but it's not exactly a satisfying substitute."

Laurel nodded again and studied the waking city as they drove down Atlantic. "I'd like to come watch you fight again," she said. "Is there a Saturday night when Pam's not going to be there?" She'd put off thinking about sharing this man pretty well until now.

"I can talk to her on Friday, tell her to take Saturday off."

She nodded, the politics of the thing feeling uncomfortable and awkward. "What time does it usually start? Right at eight?"

"Pretty close. But I never fight before nine, nine thirty. I'm like one of the main-event type guys, I guess. They do all the younger guys first, the more amateur kids. Not that I'm a pro or anything."

"Are any of the guys who fight there pros?"

"Sure. Not, like, *major*, but we've got a few regulars who make some money off it. There's a guy from Dorchester who won the Golden Gloves a couple years ago, middleweight. He gets some paid fights. Gets his ass kissed and his balls cupped when he comes back to town."

"Do you ever fight him? Oh, or are you in different weight classes? You must be a heavyweight."

He raised an eyebrow at her. "You been doin' your homework?"

She grinned, busted. "You've got to weigh at least two hundred pounds."

"Two-eighteen. And weight classes don't count for shit in that gym. Everybody just steps in with whoever else is up for it. Within reason. And yeah, I've fought him."

"Wow." She looked him over again, wishing she could see his arms. "What class would I be, if I boxed?"

"What are you, like a hundred and twenty?"

One-thirty-two, but Laurel nodded.

"Featherweight, depending on who's running the fight. Why? You wanna learn?"

"Ha—no, thank you. I can't even stand to get into arguments with my roommates over the dishes. Confrontation gives me hives." She realized with disappointment that they were nearly at her building.

"Coulda fooled me," Flynn said. "You sure came on strong in that sub shop."

She shrugged. "You don't scare me."

He pulled up to the curb and leaned over, close. "Never?"

"Well, sometimes. But only in a good way."

He grinned indulgently then pecked a hard kiss on her temple. He sat back with a little *mmf.* "You smell like something. What is that?"

"Something bad?"

"Hell no. Something awesome."

"Beats me. Probably some sex pheromone."

"Maybe," he said. "Well, I got to get to work. Come by this Saturday. You can ice my bruises."

She rolled her eyes at him and unstrapped her seat belt. "I'll see you later."

When she crept through the front door of her apartment, Laurel was surprised to be greeted by Anne's round, expectant face.

"What are you doing up?" Laurel asked, looking to the microwave clock.

"What are *you* doing, just getting home?" Anne grinned, blue eyes full of gleeful suspicion. She was by *far* Laurel's favorite of her two roommates. Christie had morphed into some mutant *Ally McBeal* wannabe since discovering her brand-new life-long dream of going to law school.

"I was…out," Laurel offered, dropping her bag on the counter.

"Who with?"

"Just a guy."

"You've got sex hair," Anne said, doing her mischievous little thumb-biting thing, practically glowing with triumph.

"I've got *messy* hair," Laurel corrected, mussing it further with her hands. "That's all. And me and my messy hair need a shower."

"You smell like…" Anne came in close for a whiff. "Like the nastiest cocktail ever invented."

"It's Bactine." She hoped that wasn't what Flynn had smelled in the car.

"Are you boning a he-nurse?"

Laurel pushed her shoes off, resigned to the grilling she frankly owed her friend after months of romantic flatlining. "It's nothing to get excited about. It's nothing serious or anything." She ignored Anne's skeptical eyebrow. "And what *are* you doing up so early?"

"The smoke alarm went off again. Four fifty-two in the frigging morning. You might've got away with your little midnight rendezvous if I hadn't barged in there to see if you were on fire. You want coffee?"

"God yes."

Anne pulled the canister out of the fridge. "So let me guess. It was so bad you caught the T as soon as it started running? I hate those mornings."

Laurel was tempted to run with the proffered excuse and be done with the conversation, but she wasn't much on lying. "No, he gave me a lift. He just works really early."

"How was the sex?"

"Who said I had sex?"

Another accusing eyebrow.

"Fine. The sex was great, actually. He's just not, you know, boyfriend material."

"What's wrong with him?"

"Depending on whose criteria you're going by, a lot. But I think he's all right. He's just not in the market for that. It's not an exclusive thing."

Anne filled the pot and flipped the coffeemaker on. "Sounds sordid."

"It is, actually, and that's exactly how I want things to be right now."

"I like this new liberated Laurel. You working today?"

Laurel nodded then yawned. "Not 'til one."

"Job searching this morning?"

"Sadly," she fibbed. She wasn't above a fib. She'd been blaming her delay in diving back into the engineering pool on the crappy state of the economy, but really the mere idea of it made her sick to her stomach. "Not getting my hopes up though." She wandered to the fridge, read Christie's latest passive-aggressive Post-It then rolled her eyes at Anne. "We're labeling our butter now?"

"She must be boning up on dairy liabilities." Anne's ability to shrug off other people's psychoses was her most admirable trait. She set two mugs on the counter and Laurel stood the half and half carton beside them. They both crossed their arms and stared at the burbling coffeemaker.

"So can you tell me *anything* about your mysterious new conquest?" Anne asked.

"He's tall."

"Okay."

"And he's from here," Laurel said. "And he's kind of a meathead."

"Wow, sounds savory."

Laurel nodded. "He's gawt a wicked heavy accent."

Anne pulled the pot out before it was done brewing, drops of coffee hitting the burner with a sizzle, another offense Christie would surely want to make note of. "Pissah."

"Yes indeed." Laurel grinned as she poured cream into her cup and earned herself a nudge in the ribs.

"Look at you, Little Miss Smiley. I'd like to meet the guy who made you do that for the first time in, like, a whole year."

"Don't hold your breath."

They took their coffees into the living room and Anne switched on the TV, scanning through her roster of recorded shows. "Is six a.m. too early to watch *The Bachelor* and mock all the giggly, desperate women?"

"Go for it. Though I bet it'd work better as a drinking game," Laurel said. "One shot for the flirty arm touch. Chug if they strip and bum-rush the pool."

Anne hit play. "Like they'd get their hair wet."

Laurel stared at the screen, laughed at Anne's comments but felt another pang jolt her insides. "Would you say this show makes something incredibly complex—you know, relationships—into something mind-numbingly vapid? Or does it make something actually rather simple into a big fucking circus?"

"Both. That's why I love it."

"I couldn't stand competing for a man like that," Laurel murmured. "I don't have the right…programming for it. Like to fight like that. Some people get an adrenaline rush and they're like *foosh*, give me somebody to beat down. I just, like, curl up into a ball and want to hide."

"I'm somewhere in the middle," Anne said. "I'm like a ninja. I'll, like, swoop down from my shadowy perch and beat you down, bitches. You won't even see me."

"The guy…"

Anne's head turned a fraction. "What about the guy?"

"He's a fighter," Laurel said. "Like, a boxer."

Anne swiveled bodily to face Laurel, almost comically impressed. "Oh shit, that is *sexy*. Is he all, you know?" She mimed some Hulk Hoganish flexing, a funny look for a heavy girl.

Laurel nodded.

"Well done you."

Laurel watched a blonde having a meltdown on the TV, confessing her never-ending but tragic love for the show's sole male to the camera, to millions of viewers. "Like I said, it's not anything. I mean, look at that chick. Even if it was an option with this guy, I'm just not up for all that. All that messiness."

"You're way less of a spaz than her," Anne said. "I so hope he ditches her next. Or actually, no. What am I saying—where's the fun in that?"

Laurel took a sip of her coffee. "Anyhow, it doesn't matter. This one's not exactly the guy you'd bring home for Christmas."

"Ah. Jewish?" Anne teased, then jerked her head around. "Is that you?"

"What?"

"Is that your phone?"

Laurel strained to pick out the sound of her ring over the television. She abandoned her mug to jog to the kitchen counter. The last name she'd have expected blinked on the screen.

"Hello?"

"Hey, sub shop girl."

She moved to the far side of the room, keeping her voice low. "Hey. I thought you didn't do calling."

"I assumed you were beyond the potential freak-out stage. Was I wrong?"

"I guess not. What's up?"

"I'm at the Dunkies by my site and I figured out what you smell like."

Laurel made a noise only she heard, a little laugh caught in her nose. "Oh. What's that?"

"That gooey stuff inside a Boston crème donut. That's what you smell like. Now I'll get a hard-on every time I eat one."

She snorted. "Did you just call to sexually harass me?"

"I'm allowed now, ain't I?"

"Go to work, Flynn. Go...go drink some decaf."

"Yes, ma'am." Laurel heard a smile in his voice before he hung up.

She switched her phone off and aimed a goofy smile at the kitchen sink, composing her face before heading back to the living room.

Anne batted her eyelashes demurely as Laurel flopped onto the couch. "That was him, wasn't it? Your mister he's-not-anything."

"So what?"

"So you are so doomed, Laurel. It looks like a rouge factory exploded on your face."

"Stupid traitorous complexion."

"I think it's cute. I think you like him."

Laurel pointed her eyes at the screen, as stony as she could manage. "Shut. Your butt."

"Oh man, you have it bad. I bet his arms are like…" Anne cupped her hands as if she were trying to grab hold of an Easter ham.

"Silence, please? I'm trying to watch this documentary." Laurel nodded at *The Bachelor.* "I believe one of the females is about to present to the alpha."

"Fine," Anne sighed. "Be that way. But don't think for a second you're any good at hiding that shit-eating grin."

"I am cool as a cucumber," Laurel said loftily.

"Bitch, you are fucking doomed."

CHAPTER SEVEN

WHEN LAUREL DESCENDED the metal steps to the gym on Saturday night, the smell left her dizzy. Enjoyably so.

She found Flynn still dressed in street clothes, talking to the same young ref from the week before, demonstrating some combinations in the air between them. She walked over, waved as she caught Flynn's eye. He gave the kid a clap on the shoulder and he and Laurel were left alone.

"Hey there, sub shop girl. You're early. It's barely seven-thirty."

"Both my buses came really quick." Technically true, though more accurately she'd *left* early, wanting the pre-fight time to hang out with Flynn, to see how he changed from the start of the evening to the end. And to be seen with him.

"Well, make yourself useful," he said. "Come on."

He led her to a metal rack loaded with free weights, grabbing one in each hand and nodding to indicate she should do the same. She selected a smaller pair, fifteen pounds apiece, and followed Flynn, shuffling behind him into a side room cluttered with workout equipment. They steadily emptied the rack of dumbbells then carried it to the room, shutting and locking the door.

"They should really just put wheels on that thing."

"Want to get the beer station set up?" He pointed to the folding table leaning against the far wall, plastic bags of Solo cups and a keg sitting beside it.

Laurel got busy, pleased to be a part of the evening, a part of the gym. Part of some secret, shady club, so much more interesting than her own life lately. Once done, she wandered to where Flynn was chatting with another fighter, a stocky guy already dressed in shorts.

"I can't lift the keg by myself," she said and offered a little wave to the other man.

"Laurel, Jared, Jared, Laurel," Flynn said, and they shook hands before Flynn walked to the beer table with her, hefting the keg while Laurel basked in the glow of having been introduced, of being someone worth introducing.

"That closet's full of folding chairs," Flynn said, nodding to a corner. "You want to stack about twenty of them against that bare wall?"

"I don't see you doing much work for this boxing co-op," she teased.

His brows rose. "The minute you start gettin' punched in the face for everybody's entertainment, I'll quit bossin' you around."

She stepped close. "I like when you boss me around."

He smirked. "Then you just keep up the bitching and you'll get what you like."

She headed to the closet so he wouldn't see how broad her grin grew. By the time she finished arranging chairs Flynn had disappeared and come back changed, same T-shirt but wearing track pants again, and running shoes. People were trickling in, boxers warming up. Flynn grabbed two chairs and carried them to his little corner. He and Laurel sat side by side in comfortable silence, watching as everyone's excitement primed.

"Which is better," she asked, "Friday or Saturday?"

"Saturday. More folks come, and that's the night when the virgins—the first-timers—get to step in. Friday night's just for regulars, and newcomers only get to watch. The energy's way better on Saturdays. Fresh blood."

She laughed. "How old were you when you first fought?"

"Here?" He squinted into the middle distance, thinking. "Maybe twenty-four."

"What about the first time you ever fought somebody else, anywhere?"

He frowned. "Shit, I dunno. When I was six?"

"Wow, aggro much?"

"You ever been in a fight?" he asked.

"Not a real one... But I did get detention for kicking Shelly Walker in the butt with my muddy boot when I was in sixth grade."

Flynn laughed. "What'd she do to deserve it?"

"I think she badmouthed Joey McIntyre or something. I was a *hardcore* New Kids fan."

He snorted. "I hope it was worth it."

"Oh yes. Nobody puts Joey Mac down and gets away with it."

"You're a passionate woman, sub shop girl. Your parents give you hell for it?"

Laurel worked hard to keep her smile from drooping too noticeably. "Nah, they didn't care." She was relieved when the fights kicked off. Two guys in their twenties climbed into the ring, one tall, one not so much, both pretty slender and ropey.

"Are either of these guys newcomers?" she asked Flynn.

"Guy in the red shorts is a virgin. He'll win though."

"How can you tell?" she asked.

"Because the other guy's scared."

"He doesn't look scared."

"Watch how much he swallows and blinks," Flynn said, "and how tight he's got his shoulders."

She studied the man a moment. "Huh. Okay, yeah, I see it."

"Plus he didn't even warm up. When a young guy doesn't warm up, it's because he's already decided he's going to lose, so he doesn't try. Like if he tries and loses, it's worse than just saying 'fuck it' and pretending he doesn't care what happens. Fuckin' pathetic."

"Do you hate quitters as much as you hate impatient people?"

Flynn smiled. "I try to hate everybody equally."

He was right about the match. The spectators made a noisy show of heckling the young fighters but the newcomer earned an easy victory and scattered, half-assed applause. The crowd multiplied as the clock crept toward nine and Flynn stood, stripping off his shirt and tossing it on top of his gym bag. Laurel gave his prep routine her full attention, ignoring the action in the ring.

She watched him winding tape around his palms and wrists. "You have no clue how manly you are, do you?"

He cocked an eyebrow at her but didn't reply.

"Are you up next?" she asked.

"Yup." He tossed a few punches in the air, stretched his arms and back and jogged in place.

"Who are you fighting?"

He peered around the relative darkness, still jogging. "Not sure. Never sure until you step in there. You turn up and they give you a few slots, don't tell you who you're up against."

"Is there anyone you're afraid to fight?"

Flynn stopped jogging and gave her a supremely patronizing look. "You want me to find you a dull blade so you can just hack my nuts off?"

"No, just curious. You're not afraid of anybody?"

"Like I'd tell you if I was." He waved an arm around the basement. "You might as well open up a vein in a tank full of sharks, talkin' about fear around these guys."

"Oh. Sorry."

He shrugged and Laurel sensed she'd made a faux pas, touched a nerve if not insulted him outright. She bit her lip, feeling stupid.

"Don't look like that," Flynn said. "You're still getting your brains fucked out when we leave here, kiddo."

She blushed and grinned down at her hands. She jumped as Flynn surprised her, grabbing her arm and pulling her to standing. He took her face in his cotton-wrapped hands and claimed her mouth in a deep, territorial kiss. He broke away looking mean. In the ring, the ref called a winner.

"You're up," she said.

He nodded and grabbed his gloves from the ground, ripping apart the Velcro straps that linked them together.

"Aren't you supposed to wear a mouth guard?"

"This place isn't much on rules." Flynn tugged on his gloves. "That's why I like it."

She frowned. "That's just stupid. You could get your teeth knocked out."

He gave his neck a stretch that popped something audibly. "I hate those things. They make me feel like I'm chokin' on something."

"Guess I'll never get you into a ball gag, huh?"

Flynn met the remark with a sneer. "Keep that snark up and you'll get yourself punished, missy."

She offered a sarcastic quaking-in-my-boots pantomime and he punched her gently on the shoulder before wandering to ringside. Laurel studied his back muscles and triceps and tried to guess if he got nervous before he boxed. She suspected not.

The ref shouted over the din. "Next fight!"

The crowd murmured, air crackling with anticipation. With bloodlust.

From the other side of the ring, Flynn's opponent approached. They climbed up and over the ropes at the same time and Laurel felt her stomach fold in on itself.

The other man wasn't as tall as Flynn but probably weighed a few pounds more, some of it muscle, some straight bulk. He looked about twenty-five, with bleached blond hair and dark roots and sharp, closely spaced eyes that lent him a weasely quality. They tapped gloves and backed into opposite corners. Flynn's posture changed, shoulders hunching, feet shifting restlessly.

The ref whacked the bell with a wrench and the match was on. Flynn straightened up, dropping his guard and acting casual as the two fighters circled. The other man looked punchy and eager and took the offensive for the round, coming fast at Flynn a few times and threatening some jabs. Flynn kept himself relaxed, pulling his head back from the strikes but leaving his guard largely open. After a minute of this the crowd got impatient, as did the blond guy. The second he made a real rush, Flynn got serious. He snapped his fists up, tucked his chin low. Unlike when he'd fought the big black guy the week before, he didn't take any hits on purpose. He dodged and blocked until the bell rang to end the round, not having thrown a single punch of his own.

Laurel met him at his corner with water.

"Thanks." He downed half of it and handed the cup back.

"You gonna do something soon?"

"When I'm good and ready." He offered a smug grin that heated Laurel's insides like liquor.

The next round was much the same as the first. Flynn continued to hold back, his inactivity pissing the blond guy off as the seconds wore on—Laurel could see from the twitch of the man's jaw that he was getting tweaked. Toward the end of the three minutes he lost his cool. He came at Flynn with his whole body, a torrent of powerful but graceless punches. Flynn blocked a couple and took a hard hook to the neck and jab to the nose, then came back with a combination that pummeled the blond guy's chest and temple with two wet thwacks. The guy dropped to his knees for a short count, finding his feet seconds before the bell rang. Flynn knocked his gloved hands together, aiming a look at his opponent that Laurel couldn't make out. The ref rang the bell again and both men retired grudgingly to their corners.

"'Bout time," Laurel said as she gave him his water.

"You can't rush a symphony like this."

She shook her head at his grand tone, pretending to disapprove. Flynn crossed his arms on the rope and gazed down at her, so casual they might've been waiting on a subway platform.

You are some fucked-up kind of magical, she thought.

Flynn handed the cup back and donned his glove as the bell sounded to signal the third round. He didn't waste the final three minutes. Laurel wondered if he had some philosophy to prove…that a good fighter only needed one round to lay another man out. Or maybe this was a big fuck-you to his opponent, letting him know he didn't think the guy deserved a full fight's effort. At any rate, he didn't need the final three minutes. He needed just over two, when a terrifying right hook snapped the blond guy's head to the side, left him staggering a few paces until he toppled, legs buckling.

The normally surly crowd offered the most enthusiastic applause Laurel had heard yet. She clapped awkwardly with the cup in one hand, eyes on the fallen man. He blinked groggily after a half a minute but didn't make it to standing before the ref called the fight and thrust Flynn's arm into the air. Flynn helped his opponent to his feet, rewarded with a sour look as the man yanked his arm away. They exchanged a couple words Laurel didn't catch. Flynn ducked between the ropes and hopped heavily to the concrete floor.

"Well done," she said, handing him the last of the water.

He raised the cup in a weary toast and drained it. They walked to the corner together and he let her blot his sweat-beaded forehead with the towel.

"Do you ever lose?" she asked.

"Not a lot, but sometimes. Few times a year, sure. I've been doing this since I was twelve, so I'm pretty good." He touched his fingers to a clot of blood at one nostril, opening the flow and frowning at his red fingertips.

"Oh gross," Laurel said, wincing. "And twelve? Really? Is that even legal? Well, I guess if karate's legal…"

"That kid over there?" He pointed at the teenaged ref. "That used to be me. So fucking eager and hardly anybody around small enough to fight. My sister's ex, Robbie, he managed a gym in Southie way back then. He let me hang around because he was so nuts about her, and she thought it'd keep me out of trouble."

Laurel stared at the kid, feet at the edge of the ring, hands wrapped around the top rope, antsy as hell. "Did you ever want to fight professionally?"

"Nah. I'm too territorial to ever leave this neighborhood to go on the circuit."

"Really?"

"I think so. Why, you plannin' on marrying me and dragging my ass down to Providence to make babies?"

Laurel's mouth fell open and she felt her cheeks burn. Flynn laughed at her shock and gave her a clap on the shoulder. "You're too easy to freak out, kiddo."

"No, I'm not."

"Yeah, you are. It's cute." He stared into the basement's dim chaos. "Think you'd never been flirted with before."

"Not about marriage. Not by a man who's actively bleeding." She scowled at him and dabbed at his nose with the towel.

"Yeah, well, it's cute that that scares you when all the other shit I've done to you doesn't. Makes my heart all fluttery." He smirked at her. "Mrs. Laurel Flynn. Nice ring to it, don't you think?"

She wasn't sure what to say to that. Part of her was flattered he wasn't afraid to tease her about something so serious, but mostly she felt insulted. There wasn't a doubt in her mind that she and Flynn wouldn't ever go beyond regular fuckbuddies, but the fact that he could snark about marriage stung... Not that she'd been bookmarking dresses online or anything. But a bottle of conditioner to keep in his shower, maybe, some tiny symbol of her significance...? *Idiot.*

But she shrugged off her angst, determined to enjoy herself. So what if Flynn didn't belong only to her? She could always ask him not to mention that he had another lover if it kept hurting.

She didn't want it to hurt though. She wanted to not give a shit, to be as well-adjusted and relaxed about their arrangement as he was.

Laurel went through all the same motions for the rest of the evening's matches, joking with Flynn, fetching his water when he was in the ring, clapping when he inevitably won his second and third fights, inventorying his fresh injuries. The bitterness faded and she found herself excited and happy again, happy just to be here, miles outside her comfort zone but seeming to belong somehow, among all these sweaty, battered ruffians and bloodlusting voyeurs, permanence and significance be damned.

Flynn changed back into his street clothes around twelve thirty and they left, the back door closing behind them and choking off the din of other men's violence.

They walked to Flynn's building without speaking and he punched the floor buttons for two and five. He made his usual stop to knock on his sister's door then returned, a hardness to his expression.

"You okay?" Laurel asked.

"Second we get in that apartment," Flynn muttered, "it's on."

"What's on?"

The growl in his voice was all the answer she needed. "You fuckin' know."

CHAPTER EIGHT

LAUREL HELD HER BREATH the whole way down the hall, heart hammering as the door shut and deadbolt clicked. She turned to face Flynn. He tossed his bag by the door and approached her with slow, even steps. She swallowed. His eyes looked wild in the faint light leaking in from the city.

"Michael," she said. "Sorry. I just *really* need to use the bathroom. Hold that glare."

She peed and tried to gargle away her beer breath with a mouthful of tap water, checked her makeup and stepped back out into the dangerous dark. The absence of the bathroom light left her momentarily blind and she gasped as a hand grabbed her wrist and twisted it behind her back, rough, nearly painful. Flynn had taken his shirt off—she felt his damp skin plastered against her bare arm as he leaned down to speak just behind her ear.

"Scream and I swear I'll kill you."

The blood drained from Laurel's face and fingers, her extremities going numb as her pussy clenched and flooded with heat.

He smelled dangerous, like sweat and blood and dirt, and she forgot how to breathe. She found the barest squeak of her voice as his hand tightened around her wrist.

"Don't," she whispered.

"Don't what?" He pushed her, walked her roughly to the bed, forcing her down onto her chest, legs hanging over the edge. He let her wrist go to reach beneath her, both hands tugging at the button of her jeans. Adrenaline shot through her veins, mixed with her excitement, made her tingle with aggression and fear. She thrashed, flailing onto her back and wedging her feet against Flynn's stomach, trying to push him away, determined to make him work for it, wanting to feel the power and danger of his strength.

He yanked her jeans down her thighs and off her calves, hooked her around the waist as she made it to her feet and tried to bolt. His arm half-knocked her wind out and in a blink she was on her back on the bed again. Flynn's knees pushed between hers, one hand unbuckling his belt as the other pinned her by the shoulder. His broad, black silhouette blocked out the jaundiced glow from the windows and made him seem anonymous, deepening the pulse throbbing between Laurel's legs.

She slapped his arm with both hands, buckling it a moment with a hard hit to the inside of his elbow.

"Bitch." He ignored her next strikes, finishing with his pants and wrestling to get her wrists in his grip. He'd gotten his hard cock out—Laurel felt it straining along the crotch of her panties as he brought his body down to hers. He made a deep, hungry animal noise that raised the hairs all down her arms. She yanked and pushed as hard as she could, barely budging him.

"Don't make this harder than it needs to be." He held both her wrists in one fist, pinning them above her head as he reached for the shelf. He ripped the condom open with his teeth and got it on so fast

Laurel could only marvel. She forced herself back into character, bucking her body under his.

"Fucking lay still." He reached down and pushed the crotch of her panties to one side, big fingers finding her pussy wet and ready. "Oh yeah, you're gonna feel beautiful."

Two fingers slid in deep, thrusting, and Laurel did what she hoped was a convincing job of feigning disgust and terror. He had her pinned so well she couldn't move anything but her head more than an inch. She did the only thing she could—spat in his face.

Flynn froze and she was suddenly glad she couldn't see his expression.

He held both their bodies so still his flaring breaths rang out like shouts in the dark. Anticipation held court until finally he lowered, fearfully slow, covered her mouth with his as his hand left her panties to clasp her jaw. He forced his thumb between her lips, got her teeth apart even as Laurel bit down as hard as she dared. His tongue slid into her mouth, finding hers and giving her as explicit and dirty a kiss as he could manage. He pulled away, keeping his face close, pressing his forehead to hers and sliding his thumb free.

"You don't wanna know how rough I can play, girl." His lips brushed hers. "Now I'm gonna let your hands go and you're gonna be good, or else I'm gonna be real bad. You got that?"

"Don't do this."

Flynn ground his rock-hard cock against her pubic bone. "You didn't give me a choice, bitch."

He released her numb hands, leaned back and pulled her underwear aside again. She felt the head of his cock pressing hard between her legs, seeking entrance. Laurel hauled off and slapped him dead across the face, harder than she'd ever hit anyone in her entire life. The noise must have been scarier than the force, as Flynn's head barely moved. A snort that belonged to a pissed-off bull hissed from his nose.

His whispered words were deadly calm. "You are so fucked."

Laurel grabbed both his arms as he angled his dick and pushed inside. Fuck, he felt amazing. She stifled a moan as he forced his way into her clenched pussy.

"You're so tight when you fight me, girl." He took the whacks and slaps she laid on his arms, all his energy focused on the penetration. He eased in slow, halfway, then pulled back and rammed himself home.

Laurel cried out, the surprise all real.

He made a filthy, satisfied noise and thrust again. He yanked his arms out of her grip and grasped her wrists, pinning them together again above her head, one hand free to wrap around her throat.

"Tell me you love it," he ordered.

Laurel gave a good thrash then froze as the hand on her neck tightened. Not hard enough to choke but plenty hard enough to intimidate.

"Tell me."

She swallowed, the motion thick and labored under his palm. "I love it."

"I thought so. Tell me how I feel, bitch."

She whimpered, the noise utterly authentic. "Hard," she managed to say.

"What else?"

Another thick swallow. "Big. And long."

"Yeah." He pumped deep, seeming to luxuriate. His hips felt powerful, thighs strong and hard, spreading her wide. He released her throat, took a wrist in each hand and held them on the mattress at either side of her butt. Laurel wanted to drown in the grunts that punctuated each rough thrust. She kept her arms tugging and her pussy clenched and kept her ecstasy to herself.

After a couple minutes' hard fucking Flynn released her tingling hands, pulled out, lifted her legs and flipped her onto her stomach.

He yanked her panties down her legs and pinned her thighs together with his clothed knees. His hands found hers again, bringing them together at the small of her back, forcing her head to one side. She was too turned on to muster much of a fight, just moaned as his dick brushed her butt, slid between her thighs and plunged back inside. His zipper scraped against her ass.

"God yeah." He sounded close to release, the words strangled, his body losing coordination. Laurel felt drops of sweat land on her back and wished she could see that hard body working, all those glistening muscles and his angry cuts and bruises.

"Oh fuck, I'm gonna come. Fight me, bitch. Fight me."

Laurel did her pathetic best to struggle and whatever little resistance she managed was enough. He pounded hard for a half minute and came apart, hips hammering as he groaned through his release.

She expected him to collapse but the opposite happened. He let her go and rolled her onto her back, ditched the condom and curled his body beside hers. She relaxed her head into the pillow as his hand found her pussy. He dipped two fingers inside to wet them then teased her clit, fast and frantic.

"Oh God—" His mouth cut her off, claiming hers rough and deep. She touched his face, his damp hair and skin, let her legs twitch as his hand set her on fire. When the kiss broke apart she watched his slick arm flexing to pleasure her, the contour of his side and hip and jeans-clad ass in the ambient light.

"God, don't stop."

He rubbed harder, bringing the pleasure to a boil.

"Use your thumb," she stammered. "Fuck me with your fingers."

He tucked his body closer, got two fingers inside, then three, then all four, thrusting, and finally pressed his thumb to her clit.

"Flynn. God, fuck me."

"Come on, girl. Come on." He circled her clit, the touch so intense she felt a wall form between her mind and reality. Pleasure jerked her deep into the climax, bubbled up from her core and spilled into her arms and legs and out of her mouth in a long, wild moan. His hand slowed as her clenches became twitches, until the last drops of orgasm were wrung from her quaking body.

Her breath rang out in the quiet room, then her voice. "Holy fuck."

Flynn slid his fingers out, wiped them on the bedspread. His warm, slippery chest pressed against her as his arms wrapped around her waist. He rested his mouth against her collarbone and a long, satisfied sound oozed out of him to heat her skin.

"Shit, you're so hot."

Laurel giggled, smiling up at the ceiling. "You're real pretty yourself."

"Let's quit our jobs and fuck all day."

"Works for me. Think somebody will subsidize that? Maybe we could apply for some kind of research grant."

Flynn made a happy noise and his arms tightened. They lay quietly for ten minutes, until their collective breathing was even, sweaty bodies cooled. Flynn pulled away, got to his feet, wandered across the apartment to switch on the lights. Laurel sat up and watched him puttering, tossing clothes from his gym bag into a hamper. He disappeared into the bathroom briefly and the sound of the shower left her sad, made her wish his smell wasn't being washed away. He emerged shortly with a towel wrapped around his waist, hair dripping. She studied his body, those familiar injuries like angry, transient tattoos.

She rolled herself off the bed, went to the bathroom to tidy herself and retrieve some first-aid accessories. Flynn eyed the items as she approached and took a seat obediently on the coffee table.

"God, you're such a mess." She sat at the edge of the chair and soaked a wad of toilet paper with antiseptic, tilting his head up to swab his latest cuts. She smeared Bactine over the deep ones, studied his eyes under the guise of scrutinizing his injuries. He moaned as she daubed at a scrape on his throat, not a sound of pain.

He pressed his neck into her touch, spoke through a heavy sigh. "I like when you do that."

"Do what?"

"You know…" His words faded to a mumble. "Fuss over me."

"Take care of you?"

He nodded, just the briefest dip of his chin.

Laurel wasn't sure what to do with this information. It was tough to write things off with Flynn, as he so rarely made sentimental proclamations, and the ones he did make couldn't be blamed on alcohol.

She finished swabbing the scrape, blotted his skin until none of the tiny lines offered any fresh blood.

"You're a strange man, Michael Flynn."

"Can I call you Nurse White? That's such a good porno name."

She rolled her eyes at him. "I bet there isn't much porn out there that does it for you, huh?"

"Why d'you say that?"

"Because the normal stuff's probably too boring, and the things that you *are* into… Well, I guess I just imagine it would be icky, watching other people pretending to do rape stuff and all that. Or worrying if it wasn't really simulated. I mean, I feel grossed out just trying to imagine Googling the keywords for that."

"You're not far off."

"Plus I don't think you own a computer. Or a TV."

"There's a laptop around here someplace," he said, sounding suddenly sleepy and distracted. "I haul it to the coffee shop if I need to do something online."

"You know…"

"What do I know?"

"I was just thinking, when I first met you, you seemed really…obvious," she concluded. "And you're not. Not just how you are in bed," she said, rambling. "On the outside you're, like, über-macho, Mr. Toolbelt-and-Boxing-Gloves with your bossy accent and your attitude and your…tallness."

"My tallness?"

"And your body and everything. But you're really something else on the inside. Sorry," she said after a pause. "That sounded way more squishy than I meant it to. Should I insult you, to take the edge off all that squishiness?"

"Nah. I'll just take it out on you next time."

She smiled. "I'm sure you will." She eased a bandage over his nastiest cut, pressed it gently into place. "Done fussing."

He nodded.

Laurel carried the supplies back to the bathroom, took a quick shower and reemerged naked. Flynn was stretched out on the bed in his shorts. He sat up as she flipped the bathroom light and fan off. As always, his gaze lacked subtlety and, as always, she liked it.

"Can I steal another shirt to sleep in?"

He managed to stare even more pointedly. "Fuck no." But he rose a moment later and tossed her a tee from his dresser, looking disappointed as it swallowed her torso.

"Thanks."

"Hit the lights and get over here."

Laurel turned the overhead lights off, came back to the bed, dusted the grit from her feet and lay across the rumpled covers. Flynn rolled to his side, coming close. He wrapped his arms around her waist and buried his face in her damp hair, his breath flaring in hot, slow intervals.

"You said you don't do spooning," she said.

He shushed her.

"Are you the only one allowed to break the rules you make?" she asked.

"I dunno. Try sometime and find out."

They lay in silence for a long time. As Laurel grew drowsy she felt Flynn's body calm then turn restless. His sticky arms shifted around her.

"You okay?" she asked.

"Christ, your skin smells so fucking good."

Before Laurel could offer a sleepy reply she was turned onto her back and Flynn was braced above her. Her body roused a few seconds ahead of her brain. "Hello."

"Like vanilla custard."

"So you say."

He leaned in and kissed her, light and slow, a lazy drag of his warm lips against hers. "You too sore?"

"Nope. Have at it."

He smirked. "You need lube?"

"Find out for yourself."

The smile deepened and he slid a hand between their bodies, two fingers dipping inside her pussy. "Oh fuck."

He found a condom and kicked his underwear away. Laurel peeled her shirt off and watched him stroke himself stiff, knowing the mere fact he hadn't ordered her to do it marked this occasion as different. By the time he rolled the condom on, his breathing was labored, heavy and impatient. She propped her legs open as he knelt between them, his palms flat on the mattress beside her ribs. His hips angled his cock to her pussy and he sank in slow.

"God," Laurel muttered. "I love your cock."

He lowered to his elbows and pushed his face against her neck, muffling his words. "I love your cunt. You're so fuckin' warm. I can't get enough of this."

She whispered above his ear. "Do you want me to struggle?"

"No. I just want to fuck you."

She ran her hands up and down his body, admiring his back, his ass, the week-old rope-burn scar still raised along his shoulders, the damp bristle of his short hair. Eventually her palms settled on his hips. She memorized how he felt. She brought her legs up, wanting to wrap her entire body around him, possess him as he was possessing her.

He took his time, pumping deeply, savoring, giving his cock whatever it needed as his curt, hungry breaths warmed Laurel's neck.

In time his thrusts shifted, turned frantic, the change in this domineering man fascinating her. She curled her nails against his skin and shuddered at the power she felt, sensing how helpless he'd grown.

"Michael."

Flynn shot up on locked arms and froze.

"Oh God, sorry," she said. "That was supposed to be a sweet-nothing, not a safe word."

His rigid body fell slack. "Jesus, you scared me."

"Sorry. Is it okay if I call you that? Can I change my word?"

"To what?"

"Uh...parakeet?"

"Fine." He leaned in close again, bringing his slick chest back to hers, breathing into her shoulder. "I'm not used to being called that though."

"What, parakeet?"

He snorted. "No, genius—Michael. Doesn't really feel like my name."

"You'd rather I called you Flynn?"

He pushed back up on to his arms. "Yeah."

"Okay. I will. But let's keep the new safe word. In case I slip up again."

His body got back to work. The desperate quality from before hardened, transformed at least partly into his usual, aggressive style. He felt good, but she missed that tiny taste of what she suspected was a rare glimpse at a softer side of Flynn. Of Michael, maybe. But she made a mental note to not get her hopes up about seeing too much of this man's gentler alter ego.

Above her, he moaned. He hammered her deep, their thighs slapping with each pump. "Take my fucking cock."

She grasped his hips, tugging in time with his thrusts to spur him on.

"God, I wish I could fuck you bare. Come right inside you." He slammed into her then suddenly stopped, pulling out and moving back on the mattress.

"Is everything okay?"

He was already lowering himself, moving his face between her legs. "I need to taste you."

She gasped as his tongue lapped at her clit, hot and wet and hungry. He hooked his arms under her thighs and clamped his hands to the creases below her hipbones. Laurel had gotten plenty of head in her time, but never like this. Flynn *fucked* her with his mouth— tongue driving deep, lips suckling, the stubble of his jaw scraping her tender skin to fan the flames. He set a rhythm of firm licks from her lips to her clit, punctuating each with a grunted, "Yeah."

"God, Flynn."

"You taste so fucking amazing." He brought his head up and Laurel could see the violent rise and fall of his chest. "Sit on my face," he said.

She got up and they swapped places, Flynn lying back with his head just below the pillows. She swung a leg over and wedged her calves under his arms, settling her pussy against his mouth and grasping the edge of a shelf for balance. She fussed with the position until he yanked down on her hips, pulling her closer. "Oh God."

His voice was thick and desperate. "Fuck my mouth." He made his tongue stiff, spearing her, nose grazing her clit, and Laurel rocked her hips and let the sensations and textures of him drive her insane. One hand left her and she felt the motions behind her, knowing he'd started stroking himself. She let go of the shelf and leaned back, craned her neck, wishing she could see more. A flash of his pumping fist and swollen cock, the condom stripped—then her balance faltered and she faced forward again, grabbing the shelf.

Flynn broke away, and his next order unnerved her a little. "Turn around."

She obeyed, fascinated by how he still managed to be in charge, even as he served her. She got in position and tried to ignore how vulnerable she felt, spread open with her ass in his face. But as she braced herself on her palms, facing his feet, the view made it entirely worth it. Flynn's mouth went back to work, followed by his hand.

"Yes," she murmured. "Gimme a good show, Flynn." It wouldn't be hard to stroke or suck him herself, but Laurel wanted to make him do the work, to be spoiled by this bossy man. She watched that tight fist pulling on his thick cock, luxuriated in his flicking tongue and sucking lips. Her brain projected a screen over the visual and she imagined him losing control. Each time she conjured the image of him shooting, bathing his belly in all that hot come, she edged closer to climax.

When the pre-come glistened at his tip she reached out to rub it into his head, teasing his slit with her thumb, loving the moan he rewarded her with.

"I can't wait to watch you come, Flynn."

His grip seemed to tighten, the pulls slowing for Laurel's enjoyment, turning more explicit. She cupped his tight balls in her palm, squeezing, fondling, rubbing the smooth skin just behind them. His body jerked beneath her, sending her tumbling into her release. Her thighs fluttered around his face as the pleasure rocked through her. She watched that fist crank into overdrive, fucking his cock fast and rough, getting him there just behind her. His chest and stomach clenched, and the first spasm lashed come against his damp skin, followed by two more, a deep groan, then peace. He swore softly.

Laurel fumbled off of him and flopped onto the mattress. He grabbed the towel and cleaned himself up, then his body wrapped around hers again, warm and damp from the summer and the sex.

"Man," she sighed. "That visual should keep me going 'til the next time I come over."

"Pervert."

"Oh right. Me, the pervert." She reached back to pat his damp hair. "You keep telling yourself that."

They fell silent, sleep soon coming down on Laurel like a narcotic curtain. Clothes, covers and no-cuddling rules abandoned, she fell asleep to the rhythmic hush of Flynn's breathing in her hair.

CHAPTER NINE

LAUREL WOKE FIRST, sleepy morning light from the tall windows coaxing her eyes open. She peeled her body from Flynn's, still in the same positions as when they'd fallen asleep. He groaned as she stood from the bed.

"What time is it?"

She squinted at the microwave. "Nine thirty-two."

"Oh fuck." He sat up, confirmed the time and swung his legs to the floor. "This is real obnoxious, but we gotta get going."

For real? She'd been looking forward to a lazy couple of hours before she had to go home and get ready for work. "Seriously? It's Sunday."

"I know. I gotta drive my sister to frigging church." He yanked his underwear and jeans up his legs. "I can drop you at home, if that works for you."

"Okay. Sure." She dressed and threw on some mascara and concealer, frowned at the reflection of her hair, parted weirdly from being slept on damp.

Flynn looked ready to go when she emerged.

"Sorry about the rush," he said. "I don't usually sleep so late. You must have fucked the sense out of me."

The compliment took the edge off her disappointment. "It's fine. I have to work in a bit, so I should probably get going anyhow."

She assembled her purse and Flynn locked up behind them. They took the elevator down three flights and she followed him to apartment 202. Flynn knocked and female voices flared behind the door.

"They're never fuckin' ready on time." He thumped a couple more times. "Jesus can't wait all day, ladies."

Laurel raised an eyebrow at him. "What was your stance on impatient people again?"

"Punctuality trumps patience."

"And where exactly does hypocrisy fit in?"

Flynn's smirking retort was cut off as the door opened and a harried-looking woman appeared before them. She was tall and pale like Flynn but with unconvincing auburn hair and at least an extra decade's wear and tear.

"You have to pound my door so fuckin' hard, Mike?"

"It's nearly ten of. Heather, this is Laurel, Laurel, this is my sister, Heather."

Heather put out a hand and gave Laurel's a firm shake with a faint bite of acrylic nail. "Nice to meet you. Kim's just putting her face on." Heather left the door open and disappeared inside, replaced by a faint whiff of cigarettes.

Laurel looked to Flynn. "Putting her face on? I thought your niece was, like, six years old."

"That's my grandniece. Or great-niece? Anyway, that's Kayla. She's usually at her dad's on the weekends, or with his mom, at any rate. My niece Kim is twenty-two."

"How old is Heather?" Laurel asked, keeping her voice low.

Flynn did a calculation in his head. "Forty-six."

"Wow, big gap."

"There's a few more of us in between, but I'm only close with Heather."

His sister reappeared in the doorway. "Yeah, I raised his ass."

Flynn nodded. "Yeah, she raised my ass. Fine, upstanding citizen you created too."

Heather's penciled eyebrows rose dryly. "Sober, employed, no record. I did just fine, thank you."

A plump young woman materialized behind her, looking more prepared for loitering outside a convenience store than for church. Snug jeans with overdone fade marks, brassy-blonde hair pulled back in a tight bun, two long corkscrew curls hanging down in front of her ears. Her makeup suggested she was looking to make an unlikely impression on her Lord and Savior.

"Hey," she said. "I'm Kim."

"Laurel." They shook hands as Heather locked up.

Flynn led them to the elevator and a minute later they piled into his car, shotgun entrusted to Laurel. He started the engine and made a U-turn onto the street.

"So where's Ricky these days?" he asked, eyes on the rearview mirror at one of the women. No one spoke. "What's a shrug mean?" he asked. "Prison? Rehab? Cult?"

Kim spoke, sounding theatrically bored. "No. He's around."

"Around where?"

"I dunno," she sighed. "Someplace."

"He still in school?"

Another sigh, angstier than the last. "If I see him I'll ask him."

"Where's Kayla? With his mom?"

Another silent reply via the rearview.

Laurel stared straight ahead at the road, wondering how often Flynn's fly-by-night lovers drove around with his family on a given Sunday morning.

"Your eye looks better," Heather said.

"This one's been playin' nurse, takin' good care of me," Flynn said, jerking a thumb at Laurel.

She blushed, glad the women wouldn't see.

Flynn pulled up beside a stone church five minutes later.

"Thanks, Mike," Heather said. "Nice to meet you, Lauren."

"Laurel," Flynn corrected. "See you at twelve. Pray for my soul."

The women climbed out and Kim mumbled a goodbye before the doors slammed.

"Right," Flynn said. "Straight home, or you need a lift someplace special?"

"Home's fine. I have to work at one."

Flynn flipped on the radio and they drove into Boston without speaking. His silence seemed comfortable but Laurel's felt melancholy. She blamed the damp air and the flat gray sky. She turned to him as they passed the huge waterfront hotel, mere steps from where they'd met.

"I sort of get why you were so hard on that idiot couple, that afternoon I bought you lunch." As soon as the words came out she worried he'd take it as an insult, think she was calling his niece obnoxious.

But all Flynn said was, "I want to shake her sometimes. And her fucktard boyfriend."

"Is your sister married?"

He shook his head. "But they were together for a long time, her and Kim's dad—Robbie, the guy who taught me to box. On and off, but mostly on. Really good dude. They broke up maybe five years ago. I try to bust Kim's balls as much as I guess he would, if he was here."

"Was he like a father figure to you or something?"

Flynn gave a dismissive sort of snort. "No. He was just my sister's cool-ass boyfriend, who treated me like a grown-up when I was twelve. Every guy I knew whose dad was around, they made me pretty sure a father's just there to yell a fuck of a lot and to have a bottle surgically attached to their hand the second they got home from work. *If* they worked. Robbie found Jesus or something when he was like eighteen and I never saw him drink anything harder than Red Bull in the twenty years I knew him."

"Are you religious?"

He shook his head. "Not since I was about ten."

"Your tattoo looks religious," she said. She'd Googled the Latin already but decided not to share this fact in case it sounded like something a stalker might do.

"It is," he said. "It's about Saint Michael."

Laurel grinned. Archangel Michael. Holy ass-kicker.

"That's actually Robbie's fault too," Flynn said. "When I was in high school he photocopied this painting for me out of an old art history book, of Saint Michael slaying Lucifer, since he's my namesake or whatever. I think he was trying to make religion seem bad-ass."

"Maybe it worked. You did get the tattoo."

Flynn shrugged.

"He sounds cool," Laurel said. "Robbie, I mean. I'd like to meet him sometime."

"Wish you could, sweetheart, but he's dead."

She winced, taking a psychic punch to the gut. "Oh. I'm sorry."

Flynn kept his blue eyes firmly on the road. "He shot himself a couple years ago." He crossed himself in such a reflexive-looking fashion Laurel wondered if he even knew he'd done it. "Cool motherfucker though. He went with me for a school thing when I was in, like, eighth grade. I forget why but he chaperoned, and I felt like the hottest shit happening, showin' up with my sister's tattooed, welterweight boyfriend to go to the aquarium or whatever."

Laurel studied his smile from the passenger seat. "Was he much like you?"

He shrugged. "I hope I'm something like him."

"Sounds like you are. Fighter, tattoos, non-drinker."

"It's a start. Anyhow, he was in the Army Reserve and then everything went and fucked its own ass in 2001. He got shipped out, came back after a couple years, all different. Real angry. He mellowed after a while, but he was always sort of…tired after that. He always cared more about stuff than everybody else around him. Tried harder. Just gave more of a shit than everybody else. I think it fucked him up to be over there, then to come back and see everything the same here, everybody still fuckin' around, being idiots, pissing their lives away, after he saw whatever he did in Iraq."

"Ah."

"You know when you spill, like, cleaning fluid or butane on something plastic, and it takes all the shine off it?" Flynn asked. "It's like Robbie was shiny when he left, and he came back dull."

Laurel frowned at this sad scrap of poetry and watched the pedestrians as Flynn turned them down this street and that through the North End. He pulled up at her building and put the car in neutral.

He wrapped his arm around his headrest and turned to her. "When do I see you again?"

"Oh um…I'm off Wednesday night again, if that works."

He nodded. "I've got training from four to six then I'll grab some dinner and a shower, see you around eight?"

"Sounds good. Well, thanks for the ride."

He dropped his arm and leaned in, took her face in his hands and gave her a long, hard, tongue-less kiss, fingers shoved deep in her hair. "Don't you take any shit from any tourists."

She smirked at him. "Only from townies."

He ran his thumb over her chin and smiled. "Fuckin' right. See you in a few days, kiddo."

CHAPTER TEN

LAUREL SHIFTED THE PAPER GROCERY BAG in her arms and fumbled for her phone, checking its screen. Five twenty-eight. Flynn should be nearing the end of his training, but hopefully not so late that she'd miss watching some of it. She let the butterflies swirl in her middle, enjoying them. Until she reached the bar and they promptly turned to rocks.

Closed.

"Fuck." What sort of a shady bar wasn't open by this time? A man emerged from the alley, a huge white guy with a shaved head and tattooed neck and a gym bag slung over his shoulder.

"Hey!" Laurel said. "Excuse me."

His eyes met hers then took a brief trip down the rest of her body, wary but intrigued. "Yeah?"

"Is Flynn down there?" She nodded at the building.

"Yeah."

"Is there some way I can get in? I'm supposed to meet him." *In two and a half hours.*

"Sure, there's a keypad." He stepped close, looking around, his proximity and rather potent body odor making Laurel's flight instincts hum a warning. "Punch in four-nine-nine-two-two-five, then the pound key," the guy murmured.

"Thanks." She offered a smile and sidestepped him, heading down the alley. The keypad was beside the heavy metal door and she entered the code. The box beeped and a lock released. Laurel heaved the door open and stepped into the dim stairwell and that familiar cologne of sweat and Tiger Balm.

The place was different by day, still seedy and dingy but brightly lit, feeling like a gym for the first time. She lingered at the threshold. Two men sparred in the ring, wearing head gear unlike on fight nights. The fingers clutching the bag tightened as her eyes landed on Flynn. Track pants and no shirt, same as when he fought, and, same as when he fought, his body made her weak.

He was working out at one of the tall leather punching bags, throwing combinations, hooks and jabs and uppercuts interspersed with blocking motions from his fists and elbows. He'd wrapped his hands but wasn't wearing gloves. Laurel frowned, conjuring x-rays of fractured knuckles in her head. When he stopped to grab a bottle of water from the floor she walked over. He set the bottle down and went back to punching. He didn't look at her until the third time she cleared her throat.

"Oh," he said, eyebrows rising. He dropped his guard and hiked his pants up an inch, cinching the drawstring and retying it. "Hey. How'd you get in here?"

She offered a haughty little smile. "Some gigantic guy with a shaved head gave me the code."

Flynn spotted the grocery bag and took a step closer, giving her a deep whiff of his insanely good smell. "What's all this?"

"I thought I'd save you some time and money and cook dinner at your place. If that's okay." Her heart stopped at a sudden possibility. "Unless you were meeting someone for dinner or something..."

He shook his head. "Nope. Cook away."

Her pulse started up again. "Cool."

"I hope I have all the pans and things you need," he said.

"I'm sure you will. It's just chicken pot pie, and I brought aluminum pie plates."

"Shit, from scratch?" He looked impressed then leaned in close. "I hope you're prepared to get your daylights fucked out, showing up promising home-cooked meals."

"I did factor that into the planning."

He straightened up. "Fantastic. Do you mind if I finish here? I'm kinda OCD about my routine."

"Oh yes, pummel away. I'll just watch the sparring." Yeah, right. Like she'd take her eyes off Flynn when he was stripped to the waist and kicking the tar out of something.

"There's chairs in the corner," he said.

Laurel set up a seat with a good open view of the ring and a fine surreptitious view of Flynn. He finished his bag workout and headed to the far side of the gym, to the huge rack laden with free weights. It was easy to watch him through the ring's ropes, staring past the men fighting to ogle his arms as he ran through reps with dumbbells. Laurel was confident she wouldn't be able to lift the ones he used even with both hands, at least not without risking a slipped disc.

After the weights Flynn lay on his back on a bench off to one side, hooking his feet under a T-bar and doing a long series of complicated sit-ups that made Laurel's abs ache just to watch. He finished ten minutes later and walked back to her side of the gym, grabbing a towel from the ground beside his water. She hurried over.

"Can I do that?" she asked, her eagerness drowning out any fear of seeming smothering.

"What?"

"You know. Like dab you dry?"

He laughed once, hard enough to double over.

"Unless that's totally embarrassing," she said as he straightened.

"Only for you, fan-girl." He tossed her the towel. "And I like when you blush, so go ahead. Mop my sweat, you kinky beast."

She did, happily, liking that he let her. Liking that it seemed like a girlfriendly intimacy and he wasn't afraid for the other guys to see.

He left her to drag his gym bag over and pull out an undershirt.

"How often do you train?" she asked.

"Every day I don't work overtime, which is most days, lately."

"Jeez. That must be exhausting, after working a physical job all day."

"Clears my head. The dudes I'm workin' with right now are complete shits. Feels good to pound the crap out of something after putting up with those jerk-offs all day. Wanna head out? I'm all set here."

"Sure." She folded her chair and stowed it with the others, hoisted her groceries as Flynn shouldered his bag. She followed him through the back hallways and up into the sunshine.

"I hope that wasn't…weird. My showing up here."

He cocked an eyebrow at her as they came out on the sidewalk. "What, some hot woman showing up to be my towel girl? Yeah, you're really crampin' my style."

"I didn't know if there's some sort of man-code down there."

"Nah. The girls who work out there wouldn't put up with it."

"There's girls who go to your shady underground gym?" she asked, and a warm, unwelcome murmur pulsed up her neck.

"Not many, but three or four."

"They must be bad-ass."

"They are," he said.

"Have you ever, like, dated a female boxer?"

Flynn smirked at her, squinting in the late afternoon sun. "Why, you jealous?"

She answered far too quickly. "No."

"Chicks who box, you're right, they're bad-ass. They're way scarier than the dudes, and they're total pit bulls. Now think for a second what I like in a woman when the bedroom door's closed."

"Ah. Too aggressive?"

"Too many motherfuckers fightin' over who gets to wear the pants," Flynn said. "Or tie the ropes."

"Gotcha."

They paused, waiting for a WALK sign. "So never fear, sub shop girl. There's no competition to be found down there. Your alpha sub status is safe."

"I wasn't jealous," Laurel said.

He smirked again, playfully skeptical. "Could you pretend you are? Makes me feel fuckin' ten feet tall."

"You said before that on fight nights, there's not really any rules."

"Not really. Gloves and shoes, hit above the belt."

"What about steroids?" she asked. "Some of those guys are huge. Do they do any testing or anything? Do they care if people are clean?"

"Don't ask, don't tell, fight whoever's slot you draw," Flynn said.

"That seems unfair."

"It's a bar basement, sweetheart, not the Olympics."

"You haven't ever used anything, have you?" She looked at his arm, big but not in that lumpy, veiny way she associated with 'roided-out body builders.

"Nope, never. Too much of a Boy Scout."

She smiled up at the sun. "Obviously."

They walked the last couple blocks in silence and Laurel liked the stares they got. Questioning stares, probably wondering where Flynn had gotten the bruises on his jaw and arms. Nosy stares, dying to know if Laurel had bruises of her own hidden beneath her clothes, evidence of abuse. She couldn't care less what people wondered, though—she only wanted to be seen walking beside this man, knowing what his body was capable of, wishing everyone else knew too.

He pushed the elevator button and Laurel enjoyed being in the tiny foyer with him, so close to his smell and energy.

He peered into the bag again. "Can't remember the last time somebody cooked for me."

"Heather doesn't?"

"My sister spent her teens and twenties raising me and my older brother, then her daughter. I think she's all set, cooking for ingrates. Now I bet every takeout joint in Southie recognizes her voice." The elevator arrived and Flynn punched the buttons for the second and fifth floors.

"It's not a fight night," Laurel said.

Flynn shrugged and dropped his bag as the doors opened up at two. "Hold it."

Laurel pushed in the door open button and listened to Flynn knocking down the hall. A lock clicked and he said, "The sexy one's cooking me homemade chicken pot pie." Then he said, "Ow," and Laurel heard the door shut.

He returned rubbing his arm.

"The sexy one?" she asked.

"That's what Heather calls you."

"Did she bite you or something?"

"She pinched me," Flynn said. "She's always been a pincher." The doors reopened at his floor.

"You get socked in the face twice a week," Laurel said.

"You don't understand. That bitch can fuckin' *pinch*." He unlocked the apartment and Laurel carried her groceries to his counter.

"Tell me what you need," he said as he eased the lights on above the living area.

For a second she thought he meant sexually. "Oh—for dinner? Nothing. Well, a measuring cup, if you have it. And a saucepan. That's it. I'm sure I can find everything else."

She unpacked ingredients—a little bag of flour, a box of butter, chicken, gravy, vegetables, the pack of aluminum pie plates.

"I'm making three," she said. "You can keep one in the freezer and heat it up whenever." *And think about how awesome I am when you eat it.* "Three seventy-five for forty-five minutes," she added, turning to him.

Flynn was unlacing his sneakers at the couch. "Think I can handle that. I'll take a shower while you're playing housewife, if you're all set over there."

"Yup, knock yourself out."

He disappeared into the bathroom as she got the crusts made, using a pint glass in lieu of the forgotten rolling pin. Flynn came out in a towel and flicked on the radio that sat atop his fridge, scrolling until the Sox pre-game broadcast emerged from the static.

"You know," Laurel said, "this wasn't the smartest idea for dinner in July. This is really more of a winter meal."

"It's so hot when you fret about girl crap."

Her breath turned short as he drew close, wrapping his bare arms around her waist from behind.

"Smells fucking phenomenal."

"Good."

"So do you," he added, pressing his nose into the space behind her ear. Everything that had happened after Saturday's fight replayed itself in an instant across Laurel's cavewoman brain.

"I've been thinkin' about tyin' you up when I jerked off all this week," he murmured, "but maybe I'll have to replace the ropes with apron strings, after this."

She whacked the back of his hand with a spoon and he pulled away.

She sneaked little glances as he dressed in jeans and a fresh undershirt. He passed her to go to the fridge and pull out a can of something that fizzed when he opened it. The smell of ginger ale wafted past. She smiled unseen as she listened to Flynn flop onto the couch and sigh—a tired, satisfied noise.

When she'd stopped at the grocery store to pick up the ingredients she'd succumbed to a kind of easy excitement she hadn't experienced for the past couple years. Flynn had become the most enjoyable feature of her life in recent weeks. Before he'd appeared she'd been feeling restless and disillusioned. It was pathetic, maybe, but seeing him gave her something to look forward to. He offered a challenge and a change a pace, a spark of dark excitement and a taste of self-discovery after months and months of half-assed floundering. She wondered what she'd have thought a few weeks ago if someone had shown her a video of the gym and the bloodied, muscly man she'd soon after be sleeping with.

"You know," Laurel said when an ad break interrupted the radio commentary. "Every time we've hung out, you spent all day either working and training, or you spent three or four hours beating people senseless in that torture-chamber."

"Yeah."

She doled filling into each crust. "What are you like when you just have a day off? No training or fighting."

"Insufferable."

She laughed. "You must have crazy baseline energy."

"I think I'm a bit manic," he said, sounding thoughtful.

She turned to study him, his eyes lit up blue and gold in the early evening light flooding in from the west-facing windows.

"Like, really?"

"Yeah," he said. "I think so. I'm just glad I grew up after everybody started going ape-shit with the ADD diagnoses."

"You're sort of straight-edge," Laurel said.

"I suppose."

"So is beating people senseless a good substitute for Ritalin, do you think?"

"You tell me. You seem to think I'm worth cooking for." He caught her blushing then and grinned.

"Yeah, you are," she admitted, then made her expression devious. "But only because I know I'm going to get massively laid later."

Flynn laughed. "You're a fuckin' brat. And yeah, you are. Getting massively laid, I mean."

"You know…" She trailed off, needing a deep breath.

"What do I know?"

"You were talking about your friend Robbie. Who died."

Flynn nodded.

"Who killed himself." She clicked the oven on to preheat. "My mom killed herself too. A couple years ago."

Flynn's eyes widened and he stood. She prepared herself for an awkward hug but he went to turn the radio down then took his seat again. "Sorry, kiddo. That sucks."

She nodded.

"Your dad still around?"

"Yeah, somewhere, but we're not close. I never saw him much when I was growing up." She turned her attention to crimping the top crusts onto the pies.

"Brothers or sisters?"

She shook her head.

"What was she like? Your mom?"

"Sorry," Laurel said. "I wasn't trying to, like, start a conversation about it. I don't know why I brought it up."

"Because we're friends?"

"Maybe... Anyway, she was..." She shrugged, feeling a hundred years old.

"Wonderful?"

Laurel laughed, hating the bitterness anybody could hear in her voice. "No, she was really hard to live with, actually." She finished one crust and moved on to the next. "She had a really nasty kind of depression. She hardly ever could keep a job for more than a month, and she was needy and demanding and she sucked the life out of everybody around her."

"Oh," Flynn said simply.

"By the time I was ten I already knew how to forge her handwriting so I could write the rent checks. She'd go on these days-long jags where she'd lock herself in her room."

"Sounds awful."

She nodded, hating the pressure stinging in her sinuses. But she decided to tell Flynn something she hadn't told anyone, not her roommates or friends, not in any wine-soaked moment of weakness. "It was sort of a relief. When she died."

"Oh," he said again. "Did you love her?"

She hissed out a long breath. "I don't know. I don't really think so." Laurel sealed the last pie and stabbed vent holes in all the tops with a fork. "Sorry."

"Don't be. You need a hug or something?"

She kept her back to him so he wouldn't see how pink her face must be. Her lips felt thick and tight from the emotion she was holding in. "No, thanks. I *would* like some beer though. If I give you some cash would you mind going out and grabbing me a six-pack?" She turned her face halfway to meet his eyes, away from the light.

"Course. You brought dinner. You're *making* me dinner. I'll buy you whatever you want."

"Just Newcastle or Bass or something like that. Bottles."

"Sure thing."

Laurel listened as Flynn moved around the apartment then left.

She slid two pies into the oven, set the timer, wrapped the third in foil and scrawled the cooking instructions on its top with a Sharpie from Flynn's junk drawer. She made a home for it in his freezer and leaned against the counter, staring at the strip of linoleum under her feet. The pattern reminded her of her kitchen growing up. She'd play in there for hours, pulling pots and pans out of the cupboards and building cities with them on the floor. Then hunger always set in and she'd abandon her project to go in search of food. *Self-raising toddler, just add water.*

Laurel walked to the couch, gave the padded armrest a couple of lame punches and burst into tears.

CHAPTER ELEVEN

WHEN FLYNN GOT BACK they made small talk about the neighborhood and listened to the game while the pies cooked. Each swallow of cold beer loosened Laurel's throat by a degree, cooled her flushed cheeks. She felt in control of her emotions in time, steady if not relaxed.

She turned her own panic around in her head, trying to make sense of it. She thought about her mom. She thought about herself, craving a drink when she probably needed a slap up-side the head. She wondered—not for the first time—if she was depressed. She didn't linger on that final worry. It was too heavy to carry into this place, and too soon besides.

One thing did come clear, though: she knew why she was attracted to Flynn now. Attracted to being with a man who could completely dominate her in bed. It was what she'd been doing in every aspect of her life lately, wanting to hole up in the backseat and not be asked to drive. Just hand over the keys to someone else.

She glanced at him, wondering if that made him her pusher or her therapist.

They ate on the couch, finishing just as the Sox tied the score at the top of the seventh.

Flynn scraped the last of his pie from its tin. "This was fucking amazing."

"You want the rest of mine?" He accepted her dish and ate the few bites she couldn't cram in.

It felt oddly comforting to be taking care of somebody again. Somebody grateful, who could give something of himself back.

"I love cooking," she said, swirling the last of her beer around in its bottle. "Or I used to. I used to cook something good every night. Then I got out of the habit when I started waitressing and bringing home leftovers. Now I look at food and all I see is people's orders."

"Well, you can cook for my ass any night you like." Flynn cleared the coffee table and did the dishes. He looked to Laurel as he dried his hands, something cautious tightening his features.

She felt it too. Hesitation, uncertainty. They had a routine of sorts and she estimated it was eighty percent fucking, most everything else—the fights, this meal—mere foreplay. The transition into sex was complicated now, Laurel's fault for introducing a downer topic. She wished she hadn't brought it up, even if it was a relief to have told someone. But Flynn shouldn't have been that someone. As stupid and impossible as the impulse was, she wanted to be perfect for him. She wanted to be what he was looking for and that surely didn't include crying unless it was part of some fucked-up role playing scenario.

She left the couch to approach him, knowing it was her job to give him the green light but also trying to gauge exactly what she could handle without risking a meltdown and officially wrecking the evening. She put her hands on his chest, tilted her head up. He kissed her slow, soft.

Laurel made a decision to stop over-thinking everything and respect her body's wishes. She pulled away.

"Flynn."

"Yeah?"

"I'm not sure I'm up for anything too rough tonight. I feel sort of…jangled."

He nodded, leaned in, cupped her cheek and pressed his lips to the crown of her head. "No problem."

"Sorry."

"Don't be sorry. I don't look at you and just see chicken pot pies and rape fantasies, you know."

She swallowed, determined not to cry. "What do you see?"

"I dunno. Just Laurel, I guess. The smart, good-smelling redhead who's been nice enough to put up with me for the last couple weeks… Don't get me wrong, I'm thrilled to find somebody who seems to be into what I like, but just knowin' I get to have that once in a while is enough. Not every meal has to be Thanksgiving."

"You can still be bossy," she said. "I like that. I like…you know, giving up control. It feels good, not having to be in charge."

He tucked her hair behind her ears. "Sure. Whenever you're ready. Whatever you want."

"Can we make out for a while?"

Flynn extended an arm, inviting her to head for the bed and get comfortable. He kicked his shoes off and lay down beside her, and Laurel felt the tightness in her body intensify, then ease nearly to nothing. He propped himself on an elbow and smoothed her hair back from her face with his other hand, and smiled.

"What?"

"I kinda like when you're all vulnerable," he said.

"I'll bet."

"No, not like that. Just when you're all…"

"Weepy?"

Flynn rolled his eyes. "When your guard's down, I mean."

She blinked. "Do I come off as guarded, usually?"

He nodded.

"Oh."

"That surprise you?" he asked.

"Kind of." She thought of people she knew, worked with…of hyper-defensive Christie and her guerrilla Post-Its. "Do I seem prickly?"

"Nah. You just seem like you've got an extra layer on, sometimes."

"Really?"

"Not like armor, but like you're wearing an invisible sweater. Like you've got your arms crossed over your chest, even when you don't. Don't feel bad, though. This is New England, home of the cagey motherfuckers."

Even as she ached to deny it, she could feel herself tugging that psychic sweater down over her head and burying her arms in its sleeves. "I guess you're right."

"I'm always right."

Laurel didn't reply, not in the mood for Flynn's sanctimonious tone, no matter if he was kidding.

"It hit eighty-six today," he said a few moments later.

"Oh?"

"Yeah." He leaned in close, eyes watching his fingers as he played with her hair. "Too hot for that extra layer you just put on."

Laurel sighed.

"Good thing I know how to get you to take it off." Flynn put his lips to her neck.

She sputtered a derisive laugh. "Smooth, Romeo."

Flynn shut his eyes and half whispered, half sang the chorus to *Sexual Healing*. Laurel smacked him on the chest and crushed her head into the pillow, rubbed her palms over her face.

"Fine, keep your shield up. But get your clothes off, huh?" He plucked at the strap of her tank top. "You could use a distraction right now."

Yeah, right. More like *he* could use an escape from her unsanctioned show of emotion.

"Fine." She arched her back to peel the top away. "But don't think for a second that you're tricking me into believing this is some huge sacrifice you're making for me." She cracked a smile at him but looked away quick, anxious from the eye contact.

They shed their clothes and came together. Flynn's mouth tasted just like her own when they kissed, like salt and butter and gravy, and his hand against her face crowded all the worries from her head. She pulled away to stare down at his body, to put her fingertips to his ribs, to the damp skin stretched over his oblique muscles, the yellowing bruise just below his armpit. So many details, intimacies...only they weren't hers alone.

His cock hardened as her palm drifted to his belly, rousing her in turn as she felt that new power—power to excite such a strong man. She wanted him helpless for a change, revenge for how he'd made her feel the other night, teasing her about marriage at the gym, and for being tacky enough to point out her defensiveness a breath before hitting on her.

"Make me come, Flynn."

He spoke against her throat. "You want me to fuck you?"

"No. You have to wait your turn tonight."

She felt and heard his laugh, a quiet, happy noise.

"Yes, ma'am." He slid farther down the bed beside her, face at her chest, free hand creeping up her thigh.

Laurel folded her arms behind her head, intending to be as lazy and selfish as possible.

Pleasure overshadowed intention as Flynn's tongue traced a curve along the side of her breast. She brought a hand down to touch the back of his head, hummed a sigh as his lips closed over her nipple. Her fingers raked his short hair, fisted it as he suckled and as his hand edged close, teasing the sensitive crease where her thigh met her hip.

"Don't keep me waiting, Flynn."

But he did. His mouth dominated the action, lips sucking, tongue flickering, teeth grazing until Laurel writhed against him, so ready for his fingers she felt crazy.

"Touch me."

His mouth retreated by millimeters, breath cool on her wet skin. "Ask nicely."

"Touch me, Flynn, please."

His hand inched closer, the tips of two fingers glancing her lips. Her hips bucked and Flynn moaned his satisfaction against her breast. Even when he was the one taking orders, he still had all the control.

Or nearly all. Laurel surveyed his body, the stiff, beading cock at attention between his legs, surely hurting with insistence. Two big, warm fingers flirted with her entrance, his touch still slow, still light, tightening her with need and impatience. She memorized his face, the arch of his eyebrows, the bridge of his nose marred surprisingly little given how many times it must surely have been broken in the last two decades. A little white bandage next to his sideburn seemed to glow against his skin. Laurel forgot her arousal for a moment, hypnotized by him.

Fall in love with me.

His fingers pushed inside, pushed the ridiculous thought from her head. She gasped and jerked as he penetrated, two fingers thrusting then curling, caressing and teasing and coaxing the little knot of nerves inside her pussy. Shit, he was good. Heat flashed, then chills, then pure, maddening need. Tension pulsed through her veins and made her fingertips and toes tingle, collected in her belly, pounded in her clit. She felt the weight and the smooth, hot skin of Flynn's cock on her thigh, just above her knee, and imagined him ramming it in deep, all hers.

"Fuck, you're good, Flynn."

He intensified the touch, setting a steady pace he echoed with his own body, small thrusts of his hips that rubbed his erection along her leg. His mouth stayed hungry, moving to her other breast to make the pleasure burst into bloom all over again.

"Make me come. Touch my clit."

Still he made her wait. When his thumb finally grazed her hard clit she gasped, gripped his hair, raked his neck with her nails. He gave her a couple more light teases and stopped.

"Jesus, Flynn, please."

She could feel his smile from the way his lips tightened around her nipple. He pulled away, kept his fingers taunting as he got his body lower, lower, until she felt his cheek scrape her inner thigh. Two licks to her clit and the pleasure tore her apart. Heat and electricity shot through her sex, down her legs, clenching them around Flynn's back. His hand and mouth kept working, coaxed a second, borderline-painful orgasm from her, hot on the heels of the first. When he released her, Laurel watched white spots dance in front of her eyes and realized she'd quit bothering to breathe.

"Oh," she said dumbly.

"Oh?"

She melted back into the bed as Flynn lay beside her, one arm shoved beneath her head and the pillow, the other draped across her stomach, fingers fanning over her ribs.

"Hot."

Laurel mustered a wrung-out laugh and tapped her knuckles against his temple. He rested the side of his face on her sticky shoulder and she could sense his smile in her periphery.

"You're pretty pleased with yourself, aren't you?"

He shrugged, way too innocent.

"Well," she sighed, "you should be. So what would *you* like? You broke my brain, so I'll do just about anything right now."

"Nothing crazy," he said. "Just play with me, I guess."

Laurel turned her head to meet his eyes. "I can do that."

She pushed up onto her side. Flynn covered her mouth with his as her hand wrapped around his half-hard cock. That familiar heat grew against her palm, stiffened, swelled. He abandoned the kissing to stare down at her hand.

"Good," he mumbled. He rolled onto his back and Laurel sat up so she could stroke his hard belly as her other hand masturbated him. She gave him sensual, slow pulls, taking her time, loving how he changed as he got closer, how his breathing grew shallow and his face flushed, arms twitched.

"Good, Flynn."

"Harder, sweetheart. I need it rough."

"Do you need me to pretend—"

"No," he said. "Just hard and fast. I need it rough to get off."

She tightened her fist and upped the pace.

"God, yeah. Just like that. Fuck… I want to watch. In the mirror."

Laurel looked to the floor in front of the bed. The full-length was still leaning against the wall from the last time they'd used it. "Okay."

She let his cock go and Flynn got up, grabbed the comforter and tossed it on the floor. They sat down side by side, Flynn's thighs spread, inviting her hand. Two pairs of eyes watched the reflection as she resumed his torture with hard strokes. She rested her chin on his shoulder.

"You're so big, Flynn."

"Yeah."

"Look at that thick cock." She gave him slow, luxurious pulls, worshipping his length with a greedy hand. "I love it."

"I love watching your hands on me. Wanna watch when you make me come."

Even hotter than Flynn's ready cock was his face. Laurel studied his tensed features, all the evidence of his excitement and desperation. His eyes looked unfocused, hungry lips parted, nostrils flared. He dragged a hand across his flushed chest, stroking his own skin, his ribs, his nipples, his neck.

She brought her lips to his ear, made her voice sweetly evil. "You gonna come for me? Gonna let me see all that hot come shoot across that gorgeous stomach?"

"Fuck yeah."

"Oh good," she whispered. "That's what I fantasize about when I'm getting off, thinking about you." She tightened her fist to hear his moan.

"Please."

"Yeah, it's your turn to beg now," she said.

"Please. Make me come. Please." His hand moved lower, covering her small one for a few thrusts before he cupped his balls, kneading as he came undone. "Fuck, yes."

"Good. Let me see." She eased her pulls as he came, keeping her fist tight to milk every drop, watching in the mirror as it bathed his skin and feeling the wet heat slip over her knuckles. Fever flooded her face and breasts and pussy and she bit her lip just to feel the sting.

Bossy Flynn returned after a few labored breaths. "Fuck. Clean me up."

Laurel relocated, getting to her knees between his legs, leaning in to lick the come from his skin and hers. His hand cupped the back of her head, warm and heavy and possessive.

He sighed as she sat up, sounding tired in the best way. "You're staying the night, right?"

She swallowed and nodded.

"Oh good. No way I can operate a car now," he said.

They made it to their feet and he collapsed back across the bed. Laurel knelt beside him, dragging her fingers through her sex-messy hair and staring down at the length of Flynn's naked body. She'd miss this when their arrangement came to an end. She'd miss feeling like the temporary owner of this strong man, if only for an evening at a time.

She'd miss selfish things too, like how easy it was for him to get her off. He was the best lover she'd had by miles and the pain that came with knowing she'd eventually lose that shifted Laurel's mood again. Her armor didn't snap on this time. Instead she felt as if her skin were falling away, leaving her a tangle of exposed nerves and brittle bones.

She gazed out the tall front windows, wishing she wasn't flooded with ridiculous, manipulative impulses, like the desire to suddenly leave so Flynn would rush after her, try to talk her into staying.

If he would. He might not.

"What're you thinking about, sub shop girl?"

"Nothing."

"There's a vein ticcing in your neck."

She turned to frown at him, hoping she looked bored and that the hurt didn't show.

"Everything okay?"

"Yeah, just not looking forward to work tomorrow."

"Shit, I must be losing my touch if you're already thinking about work two minutes after we stop fucking."

She flopped back down against the pillows. "No, you're still the best lay of my life."

He clenched a triumphant fist in the air and they fell silent for a little while.

"Is it about what you said earlier?" he asked in time. "What you told me about your mom?"

"No."

"You want me to not ask you if anything's wrong?"

"Nothing's wrong," she said. "I'm just a bit off today."

"Would you like me to compliment your taste in shoes or listen while you bitch about your female coworkers?" he teased.

"Fuck off." Laurel pretended she was teasing back but rolled onto her side to stare at the wall, knowing her face was no good at keeping secrets. Flynn shifted a minute later, his hand closing around her arm, voice by her shoulder.

"Can I tell you something that really annoys me about you?" he asked.

Laurel frowned, confused. "I guess so."

He exhaled against her skin. "I really hate that you spent the time and money—well, somebody else's money—to get a degree you don't even want."

Her body tensed up tight as a fist. "I want my degree. I'm proud of my degree."

"How come you're wasting it then? Taking a shitty waitressing job away from some other college kid?"

A fever grew inside her, hot and defensive. She opened her mouth to reply but Flynn went on.

"You know what I wanted to do when I was little, more than anything?"

"Grow up to be an engineer?" she asked, knowing her tone was bitchy and not caring.

"Kind of. I wanted to build buildings. Not like I do now. Not hanging drywall or pouring foundations so I can end up with a bad back and no insurance when I'm fifty. Like be an architect or whatever. It pisses me off that you basically have that, and you're shitting it away."

"Engineering wasn't what I'd expected."

"And waitressing's a beautiful fucking fantasy land?"

"I stopped after my mom died, okay?" She rolled onto her back and glared at him. "For the first time in my life I decided to stop working my ass off for other people and be fucking irresponsible for a change. Happy?"

"Maybe you got depressed, like her."

She yanked her arm out from his grip. "Fuck you. I thought you hated analyzing people."

"I hate being analyzed."

"Then you must know how fucking annoying it is." She propped herself up on an elbow and stared at him in the near-dark. "It's none of your business what I do with my life."

"It's none of your business if I wear a mouth guard. But you're right to be a naggy little bitch about it."

"I'm sick of this conversation, Flynn."

"You shouldn't have said yes when I asked if you wanted to hear my opinion."

"Like you really gave me a choice. Why did you even ask me that? What was that about?"

"I wanted to know what was up with you," he said. "You went all quiet and it freaked me out. Usually when I make women go all quiet it's a really horrible sign."

"So you...you crammed your dirty fingers all inside my open wound, like I'm going to open up and cry about stuff if you antagonize me hard enough? Can't you just respect that I don't want to talk about it?"

"Sorry." His jaw clenched and released a few times. "I just wanted you to say something and stop being all shut-down. I wanted to know if I upset you."

"Well, that was a stupid fucking way to go about it."

"Sorry... Would you like to tell me something about me that annoys the living fuck out of you then?"

She squinted at him, chewing her lip. "I think it's really obnoxious that you never became what you wanted and you're being a douche about it now, taking it out on me. In *bed.*"

He nodded. "Good. We even now?"

"I also think it's irritating that you treat me like your girlfriend sometimes, when I know I'm not."

That shut him up. He didn't reply and she could see the dark circles of his irises drift toward the wall—not eye-rolling, more like escape-route-plotting.

Laurel sighed, frustrated.

"What do you *think* we are?" Flynn asked. His tone was odd, diplomatic and calm. Laurel's pulse ground to a halt.

"I didn't think you did girlfriends," she said.

"Why not?"

"I dunno. Because I'm not the only woman you're banging, for starters. Or what if another willing woman came along? You said it's hard to find people who'll go there with you. Wouldn't it be a waste to let yourself get tied down, in case a new one showed up?"

"Wouldn't it be a waste to not try and stay with one I liked?"

She entertained a dozen images in five seconds—a smiling Flynn walking down the street toward her, sliding onto a barstool next to her, shaking hands with Anne. She shifted onto her side again, staring blankly at her hand against his sheets.

"What about Pam?" she asked.

"I'm not seeing her anymore."

"Yeah, right."

"I'm not. Not since Friday, before the last time you and me hung out."

"Oh." She swallowed, hard, choking on hope. "How come?"

"Not sure. Something to do with her husband, I think. It's her business. I didn't pry."

"Oh," she said again, feeling intrigued but uneasy. "I guess that's all well and good for your little boyfriend-girlfriend speech, but I mean, would you have kept seeing her if her husband hadn't pulled the plug?"

"Not if it seemed like you and me were turning into something. Not if you'd asked me not to."

Laurel laughed, not convinced.

"You think I'm some sort of sex maniac, don't you?" he asked, voice sharp.

"No."

"You think I don't know how to date? You think the kind of sex I like is like some condition? Like a fucking dialysis machine I have to drag around behind me, making everything into a big fuckin' hassle?"

She rolled over to meet his stare. "Do you...what do you think of me as?"

"You're the nice, smart, hot, funny woman I'm sleeping with. If that's still true in a couple weeks, and maybe you throw in a night when we sleep together but don't get around to fucking...yeah, I'd probably tell people you're my girlfriend."

"I see."

"You gonna finally freak and run out the door? Let me know and I'll get my shoes on and drive you."

Laurel turned over, didn't reply. As much as she liked Flynn, as much as she liked what he was saying, there'd been a safety to imagining he'd never entertain the idea of coupledom. Now she'd inevitably look at him differently and the whole ugly dynamic of who-likes-who-more would come into play. She didn't want to wake up in a month and realize she cared more about him than he did her, that she might lose him. And she didn't know if she was ready to have someone in her life who'd hold her to a higher standard than she'd been doing herself these past couple years.

His hot sigh warmed her neck. "What're you thinking about, sub shop girl?"

"Nothing." *Tons.*

"You know I said two weeks ago or whenever that if you came and watched me fight, and you still wanted to ask me out after that, you could. We've hooked up, like, three times since then and you still haven't asked me out."

"I thought the sex counted as dates."

He made a little noise, a miniscule laugh. "Jesus. Just ask me to go out to dinner or something, somewhere besides here or the gym. Or if you don't want to, tell me now so I know where I stand. I'm happy to be your fuckbuddy, Laurel, but I'm not afraid of gettin' attached to you either. I'm a pretty simple creature."

She stared at the wall, unsure what to say or do or think.

"I'm not afraid of angry pricks kicking the shit out of me," Flynn said. "And I'm not afraid of you." He shifted, breaking their damp, sticky bond to turn her onto her back. His hand held her jaw and a thumb stroked her cheek. He brought his face down and kissed her mouth, light and sweet.

Through the rush of her quickening breath and her pounding heart, Laurel formed words, thick and fearful. "Would you like to get something to eat next week?"

He laughed. "Sure."

"Wednesday? At seven? Lucky's, on Congress?"

"Sure," he said again.

"And maybe afterward we could come back here and not have sex."

"Sounds fucking sensational," Flynn said, pulling her tight against him so she felt his hardening cock. "Can't wait to not have sex with you."

"Clearly." She swallowed, wanting to embrace the fresh wave of excitement but still distracted by the gears ticking between her ears.

"You got your force field switched on again," he said.

"Yeah."

"You said before you like how when we fuck, you don't have to be in control of anything."

She nodded.

"Let me give that to you again. Now. Let me be in charge."

"Maybe."

She sucked in a breath as his mouth closed over hers, a taste of that tempting offer. She shut off her mind, melted into what he was giving. Then a stray thought cut through the haze—a truce.

She pulled away. "If you start wearing a mouth guard, I'll start looking for engineering jobs."

His eyes flicked back and forth between hers. "Oh yeah? That a promise?"

"Yeah." She ran her hands down his body, cupped her hand over his cock. She watched his face in the low light, loving that familiar glaze to his eyes, the heaviness in his lids. "Not, like, next week. But soon."

"You keep busting my balls and I might just trick you into sticking around."

She laughed, embarrassed and flattered. Relieved.

"But don't worry, not 'til we get better at not having sex."

"That might take awhile," Laurel said, tightening her hold.

He grunted. "Yeah, probably. So don't worry, you're safe for a couple years at least. Now how about it? Let me give you what you need. Let me take you out of your head for a few minutes."

CHAPTER TWELVE

FLYNN WENT TO HIS CLOSET, returning to the bed with a short length of rope in each hand. He knelt at Laurel's feet, staring until her eyes left the ropes to meet his.

"You trust me?"

She gave it a second's serious thought, already knowing the answer. "Yes. I do."

"You want this?"

She nodded.

"Sit up."

She did. She let Flynn bind her ankles, tie her wrists behind her back—real this time, no way out. He linked her arms with enough slack that when she lay back down her fists rested at her sides, the rope between them pulled taut beneath her ass. She tested the bindings and felt a scary thrill from the sensation, true physical helplessness. The bite of the rope as she tugged was taunting, as cruel as the heat in Flynn's eyes. His knees were spread wide between her own, hands kneading her thighs. One left to move to his cock, stroking until he was stiff and ready. His gaze roamed from her pussy to her belly to her breasts, up her throat, stopping at her lips. His body followed, strong legs straddling her chest and pinned arms. He angled his cock to her mouth and brushed it across her lips.

"Taste me."

She laved him, savoring his excitement. He held himself there and she teased his slit, sucked his swollen head until she earned a moan.

"Fuck, that's so hot. You want more?"

She answered with suction, wrapping her lips tight around him.

"I'm gonna fuck your mouth," he whispered. "If I do something you can't handle, use your teeth. You know, gentle—but you let me know."

She freed her mouth enough to say, "I will."

He leaned over, braced one arm at the top of the mattress, guided his cock with the other hand. He adjusted his knees until he got the distance right.

She took what he gave her, four thick inches, sucking as his hips slid him out, then back in, setting the pace. She wanted her hands free to touch his body but accepted the frustration, made it part of the thrill. Flynn wrapped a fist around his base, either to keep from thrusting too deep or give himself pleasure, perhaps both.

"That's so good. Keep taking me. Moan for me."

She obeyed, offering a deep, thrumming noise as he fucked her mouth. He worked himself deeper a half an inch at a time and Laurel kept the suction hard, finding it eased the gagging. Flynn's hand moved to his balls. He squeezed and rubbed, making Laurel ache to touch him. She reveled in the warm weight of his thighs against her arms, the presence and energy of him.

"Yeah. Yeah. Take my cock. Suck me." He put his hand to her face, her temple, her hair. His thrusts came slow, deeper, deeper still until his head bumped the back of her throat, triggering a protest. He pulled out and rested back on his haunches.

"I like seein' you tied up, sweetheart."

Heat bloomed in her chest at those words. "Good. Do you want me to pretend I don't want it?"

"Not tonight. Right now I just want that look. Helpless and hungry."

He leaned over to grab a condom off the shelf. She watched him roll it down his cock, her body tightening as she studied all that hard muscle, hers by some filthy miracle.

"God, you look amazing," she whispered.

"You like my body?"

"Yeah."

"Good. I like when you take care of me," he said. "And I love fucking you more than you can possibly know. You make my cock feel so *fucking* big when you look at me like that." He turned her by the hip, coaxed her legs to the side, bent, shoulders still mostly on the mattress. He planted his knees wide behind her ass, a hot palm on her hip as the other hand stroked his erection.

"Fuck me, Flynn."

"When I'm ready."

"Please. Now." She licked her lips, so eager to feel him drive inside and ease the hunger.

He teased his tip up and down the crack of her ass. The hand on her hip slid between her thighs, big fingers finding her wet, getting slick before they rubbed her clit, pinching the hard nub, giving her that mix of pleasure and pain he was so good at.

"I want your cock, Flynn."

"Be patient." Wet fingers toyed with her folds, taunted with shallow exploration.

"Fuck patient. Give me your cock."

"Fine." Threat, not surrender.

She watched his face, stern and calm as he smeared her wetness between her thighs then all up and down his shaft. "Fine," he said again, barely audible.

Laurel gasped at the heat of him. Each thick inch pushed between her thighs, drove hard into her pussy until he had no more to give. He held there a full minute, letting her feel him throb and twitch, making her wait.

"C'mon, Flynn, please."

"Turn onto your side."

She shifted her shoulders, facing the wall. His dick slid out, all the way out, then rammed back in to the hilt.

"God, yes—"

A mean tug on the rope binding her wrists stole her breath. It pulled her arms back, tweaked her top shoulder and sent a little burst of pain like static shock straight down to her fingertips.

"Don't rush me," he warned.

"I need more."

Another tug, slow this time, stopping when Laurel gasped at the strain.

"You know how I feel about impatience."

She held her tongue, relieved when he let the rope go. His hands grasped her hip and waist, kept her still as he started to fuck.

He kept his composure a few moments before a harsh, hissing breath told Laurel the pleasure was undermining all that cold control.

"God, I fucking love your cunt."

She squeezed herself tighter around him, earning a fierce grunt, then a hard slap on the ass.

"Keep it tight like that," he ordered.

Laurel obeyed, making her pussy a fist, intensifying the pleasure for both of them. He spanked her again.

"Flynn."

"That's right. Say my name. Tell me who's fucking that tight cunt."

"Flynn." Each time she said it, his palm came down with another slap. By the tenth strike the sting turned savage, teetering on the threshold between pleasure and true pain. She winced, held his name back, unsure if she could expect another slap for disobeying.

Instead she felt a tug at the bindings. She steeled herself for the punishment, but after a few seconds' fumbling her wrists were free, the rope gone. Flynn's cock left her and she flexed her fingers, circulation returning as he moved to untie her ankles. She turned onto her back and he knelt between her thighs, spreading them wide, cock driving home.

"Touch me," he said.

"Where?"

"Anywhere." He was frantic, all that cool self-possession gone, his face buried against her shoulder. "Just want your hands on me."

She slid one to his ass, fisted his hair in the other. She tugged until he brought his head back and she kissed him, rough, ending with a little bite on his lower lip.

"I wanna get fucked," he moaned.

"Yeah?"

He flipped them over, lay back while Laurel found her balance, straddling his hips. She fanned her fingers over his ribs, knowing he could handle her weight as she took charge of the sex.

"God, yeah. Use me, sweetheart."

They fell nearly silent, lost in each other's bodies. A slideshow of emotions flashed across his face—need, pleasure, desperation, then warm and unmistakable fondness. He smiled up at Laurel, looking drunk.

"What?"

"You mean what you said? About looking for jobs?"

"Yeah."

He made a greedy noise and grinned, hands guiding her hips for a handful of thrusts.

"And maybe after another month or two and a fresh pair of blood tests," she added, "you might get that other wish of yours." She clenched her pussy tight and gave his cock slow, long pulls, imagining how he'd feel, releasing inside her, bare.

He grabbed her waist and moaned, pushing deep.

She watched his eyes close, his face turn helpless. And she wanted him. Wanted to be here to patch him up, to call him on his bullshit and get called out in return, to explore the darker depths of her mind and body with this patient, real, occasionally obnoxious man.

"I love when you look this defenseless," she murmured.

His voice was shallow and scratchy. "Not many women ever manage to get me on my back."

"You better keep me around then."

"Why d'you think I was so keen to tie you down?" The words hitched with his uneven breaths. "Fuck, Laurel."

The sound of her name—those two choked syllables rising from his throat as he gave her all the power... It felt like a filthy, sacred proclamation. She stared at his strained face. *Fall in love with me.*

"Laurel."

Fall in love with me.

"You keep—looking at me like that—and I swear—I'll let you wear the pants—any night you want."

She froze in mid-stroke, holding him still, locked deep inside her body. She grinned down at his sweaty face. "Beg me."

"Laurel."

"Beg me and I'll make you come so hard you'll lose your fucking mind."

He sounded as though he already had. "Please. Fuck me, please."

She eased her pussy off his cock then claimed his hard length again, rough.

"God, fuck. Please, Laurel."

"Fall in love with me." Horror slapped her in the face as the words tumbled from her subconscious into the air between them.

"I will," he grunted, still panting, still lost in the fucking.

"I didn't mean that."

He laughed. "Fine. But you keep treating me the way you have been, and I will. Whether you like it or not." He groaned. "But I won't say it in the middle of getting my brains fucked out, so relax."

She didn't reply, just kept her body moving as her mind overheated. As always, he could read her. Her fears stacked up like bricks between them but he took the wheel. He flipped them over, gave her the reassurance of the bed against her back and his weight on her body, the relief of not being in charge.

"Come for me, sweetheart." He braced his weight on one arm so he could slip his other hand between them and tease her clit. "Come for me."

"Make it rough."

He did, and when she came apart it was from his strength, his smell, his heat, the shock of that extraordinary body laboring above her. He chased her release with his own, racing home in a greedy rush, his moans filling her ears.

"Fuck," was all he said, and as Laurel couldn't sum it up any better, she concurred.

"Fuck indeed."

For a long time they lay side by side, fingers twined, breaths steadily slowing, skin cooling. Then he sat up, letting go of her hand. "Get dressed."

His tone didn't worry her. She wasn't getting the boot. She left the bed and found her panties, tugged them up her legs. Her wrists were rubbed pink, same as her ankles, and though she didn't relish explaining it to Anne, she knew she'd miss that color when it faded.

Flynn was also dressing, and they pulled their shirts on in unison.

She looked to him expectantly.

"Shoes," he said.

"Okay. Any clues, here?"

"Nope. Use the can and grab yourself a beer."

She did as she was told, emerging to find him waiting near the exit, keys in hand and a fleece throw slung over his arm.

"Late night picnic?" she asked.

"Not exactly. Hold this," he said, handing her the blanket.

"What, then?"

"Patience, sub shop girl."

She rolled her eyes but followed him out into the hall. He headed for the elevator only to surprise her, passing it and hauling open the door to the stairwell. He surprised her further when he led her up the steps, not down.

"O-*kay.*"

Up one flight to the sixth floor, and up one more, into darkness. He paused to fiddle with his key ring, switching on a tiny flashlight. Its bright LED beam bounced up the last of the steps, to where the stairs ended at a landing before a metal door. An open padlock was hooked through a latch above the handle. Flynn slid it free, tucked it into his back pocket.

The door swung open with a soft whine and Laurel found herself staring out across the old factory's vast roof. Flynn helped her navigate a steep step down, their shoes alighting on gritty tarpaper.

"This is quite a liability," she said, looking around.

"It's supposed to be kept locked," Flynn said, "but the maintenance guy smokes like a chimney up here. It'd only slow him down. C'mon."

He led her to the far edge, the side facing northwest—downtown. He took the blanket from her and lay it on the ground, and waved an arm to invite her to sit.

She did and he sat beside her, hip to hip. Laurel held her bottle and gazed out across the city lights, and neither of them spoke for a long time.

It was one of those sultry summer evenings when the temp probably wouldn't drop below the mid-eighties, but it felt good. The breeze caressed her bare arms like a lover's sweet nothings—warm and wistful, raising goosebumps. South Boston bustled six stories below, peppering the night with the far-off honk of a car, the rattle of a bus, the whir of a hundred air conditioners.

After a sip of her beer, Laurel asked, "Why are we up here?"

"To find out how we do."

"How we do…?"

"How we do, outside of that bed. How we are with each other. *Who* we are with each other."

"All right. And who are you, just now?"

"Just a guy. On a roof. What about you?"

"Just a woman. Kinda giddy. Kinda…I dunno. I feel funny."

"Like?"

"High? Weird, but in a nice way. Tiny and exposed and…naked. Up here."

"Left your sweater downstairs, huh?"

She nodded, tipped the bottle to her lips again. "I think I like it."

"You freaked yourself out, didn't you, saying what you did, in bed? When you told me to fall in love with you?"

Her cheeks burned. "It just slipped out."

"I've said way more messed up shit to you when we're fucking."

"Yeah, but that's different. That's role-playing."

"You think you were gonna scare me off?" he asked.

"Maybe."

"Don't be. Only thing that scares me is airplanes."

"I can't help it. My worries shout louder than my common sense."

He nodded. "That's fair."

"I'm… I get like that sometimes," she admitted. "I get scared, when I start to care. Caring feels like standing on the ledge of this building, almost. Dangerous. Or precarious." Dizzying, as well, with a hell of a view. "You should know going into whatever this is, I'm hardwired for depression. I keep busy and I hold it at bay most of the time, but my head can be my own worst enemy. Not always, but sometimes. It comes in waves."

"You ever been suicidal?"

She shook her head. "I don't feel despair, when I'm sad. Just…emptiness. I don't make the best friend when I'm in that space, and I doubt I'd make a great girlfriend."

"I'll be the judge of that."

"I just want you to know, after what you went through with Robbie."

"Thanks. But the way I look at it, not every day's gonna be eighty degrees and sunny. That just ain't possible. And I'm not gonna run at the first sign of storm clouds."

If only it felt that simple when Laurel was going through a dark patch… Still, a charming little philosophy.

After a short silence she asked, "What do you feel, when you're boxing?"

"Chemicals," he said simply.

"Not emotions?"

"Not in the ring. They only mess you up. All I feel in there is adrenaline and bloodlust."

"Sounds…pure."

"It is. Fighting and sex. Only drugs I need."

"Maybe I need to find that thing. That thing that shuts my brain up." The role-playing had that power. She wanted to keep exploring that, but maybe there was another way to get there, something she could do on her own. Running or drawing or spin class or meditation. Something she could lose herself in, blessedly thoughtless.

Flynn moved, shuffling to sit behind her, splaying his legs out in a V and wrapping his arms around her waist. She felt the sweet rasp of his jaw at her temple, breathed in the now familiar scent of his skin.

"Thank you," she murmured. "For this."

"Don't be ridiculous. Or actually," he said, squeezing her tighter, "be as ridiculous as you want. I'll keep buying you beer and driving your ass home."

She smiled and shook her head. "Now might be a good time to try out that mouth guard."

Another squeeze.

"You bring all your conquests up here?" she asked.

"Only the ones who cook me chicken pot pie."

"Hm."

"You staying the night?"

"Yeah."

"Good."

Laurel sighed, dropping her head back against his shoulder to stare up into the darkness, finding it disappointingly deserted. A plane blinked its way across the sky, but light pollution muted whatever grand show the heavens might be putting on.

"Feels like there ought to be stars out, on a night like this."

"There are," he said, pointing toward Boston and its countless glittering lights. "Better than stars, even."

Miles away, Fenway was still lit, a distant purple glow. The city seemed at once vast and tiny from here. The fact that the two of them had found each other in this big brick maze was really quite remarkable. "Maybe you're right," she said. This manmade galaxy was magic enough.

"Feel better?"

"I do, thanks. That stuff with my mom... It just hits me, sometimes."

"Sure. Family's a mind-fuck. Trust me, I know. Plus everything we've been doing, it takes a lot out of you. You're stripping yourself bare, way, way down past your clothes."

That was true, she supposed. She'd submitted to his appetites and his will, spread her body and mind and heart wide open and welcomed him inside. It shouldn't come as a surprise if some old vulnerabilities slipped out. The price of admission, really.

"I'm supposed to tell you," Flynn said, "there's gonna be a party next Sunday on Castle Island, for Kayla's birthday. Barbecue. Heather said you're welcome as long as you bring a side."

"You want me to come?"

"I wouldn't have told you if I didn't. And like you said about your depression, probably best if you know what you're getting yourself into from the get-go. Our family's an acquired taste."

"Nothing a couple beers can't remedy, I'm sure. I'll bring potato salad." Plus a helping of cautious optimism, because this felt very much like girlfriend territory. A few more invites like this one and Laurel might find herself in the market for a second toothbrush.

For a long time they sat without speaking, the sounds and smells of the city washing over them. Laurel felt her worries grow lighter, lighter, until they were nothing more than dandelion fluff, slipping away, caught on the sultry breeze. *The storm clouds roll in, the storm clouds roll out.* And as her mind quieted, her body grew restless.

She turned her head, temple brushing his cheek. "Let's go back down."

"You cold?"

"No." Far from it. "I want you to take me to bed."

"Do you now?"

"Show me more of what you like." *Take me way down deep into the dark. Help me find some new piece of myself there.*

He stood and helped her to her feet, and they gathered the blanket and bottle and crossed the roof hand in hand.

The things this man craved could be blacker than the sky above them, rough enough to bruise and sharp enough to sting.

And tonight they were hers to give. Hers alone.

ABOUT THE AUTHOR

SINCE SHE BEGAN WRITING IN 2008, Cara McKenna has published nearly forty romances and erotic novels with a variety of publishers, sometimes under the pen names Meg Maguire and C.M. McKenna. Her stories have been acclaimed for their smart, modern voice and defiance of convention. She was a 2015 RITA Award finalist, a 2014 *RT* Reviewers' Choice Award winner, a 2012 and 2011 *RT* Reviewers' Choice Award nominee, and a 2010 Golden Heart Award finalist. She lives with her husband and son in the Pacific Northwest, though she'll always be a Boston girl at heart.

ALSO BY CARA McKENNA

After Hours

Curio and the Curio Vignettes

Hard Time

Her Best Laid Plans

Shivaree: The Complete Series

Skin Game

Strange Love: Remastered Tales

Unbound

THE SINS IN THE CITY SERIES

Crosstown Crush

Downtown Devil

THE DESERT DOGS SERIES

Lay It Down

Give It All

Drive It Deep

Burn It Up

AS C.M. MCKENNA

Badger

AS MEG MAGUIRE

Caught on Camera

Headstrong

The Reluctant Nude

Thank You for Riding

Trespass

The Wedding Fling

Wild Holiday Nights

THE WILINSKI'S SERIES

All or Nothing

Going the Distance

Takedown

CPSIA information can be obtained
at www.ICGtesting.com
Printed in the USA
FFOW01n1433220816
27038FF